Torquere Pre

Perfect

This is a work of fiction. Names, characters, places, and incidents either are the product of the author's imagination or are used fictitiously. Any resemblance to actual events, locales, organizations, or persons, living or dead, is entirely coincidental and beyond the intent of either the author or the publisher.

Perfect
TOP SHELF
An imprint of Torquere Press Publishers
PO Box 2545
Round Rock, TX 78680
Copyright © 2004, Julia Talbot
Cover illustration by SA Clements
Published with permission
ISBN: 1-934166-45-6, 978-1-934166-45-1
www.torquerepress.com

First Torquere Press Printing: December 2006
Printed in the USA

Inspired by Perfect, as sung by Sarah Evans
For L. who thinks love should be perfect. Here's
hoping.

Perfect

Prologue

"Goddammit, Louis! If you leave that towel on the floor one more time I swear I'm gonna wrap you up in it and beat you to death."

Avery sighed. Two years they'd been living together and Louis still couldn't pick up a fucking towel. Made him crazy. Louis came out of the bedroom and looked down at the towel before looking at him.

"It's not wet," Louis said. "You told me not to drop my wet towels on the floor."

Oh, now the son of a bitch was being obstinate. "Lou."

"Yeah, yeah." Louis sighed right back and bent to pick it up. "Happy?"

"Yeah."

He wasn't. Not really. When was the last time he'd been happy? Maybe six months back, before Louis had taken a new job and had to cancel their vacation trip to Florida. Hell, maybe even after then, when he still held out hope that Louis would talk to him about the stress and the bad shoulder joint that was going to need surgery, or that the house might stay clean for five minutes after he fucking cleaned it.

Hope didn't spring eternal, though and if any man was an island, albeit a messy one, it was Louis.

"You got a beef with me, Ave?" One of Louis' heavy eyebrows went up, which was a huge show of emotion for his strong, silent type lover, and Avery took a deep breath, clutching the towel Louis had handed him.

"Yeah. I think I do. You never talk to me anymore, Lou."

"I never... Hell, I'm talkin' to you right now, Ave."

Man, sometimes it pissed him off how well those big, green eyes of Louis' did bewildered. That was just too fucking much. Lou honestly had no clue what he was talking about.

"I mean about work, or your shoulder, or anything."

Louis' expression shut down tighter than a virgin's thighs. "That's because it's none of your business."

"Yeah? Well, then I guess we're just roommates? Or maybe fuckbuddies? 'Cause I sure as Hell thought we were partners, here. That's why I've *lived* with you for two fucking years."

"Ave..." Louis held out a hand. "It's just... look, I gotta work it out first. Then we'll talk."

"Fuck that shit. That's what you said six months ago."

Crossing his arms and stepping back, Lou shook his head. "M'not getting into that Florida shit with you again, man."

"It's not about Florida, Lou. It's about you not letting me help."

"No, it's about you not understanding that I gotta handle this." Lou looked... hurt. Like he had a fucking right to be hurt that Avery was jumping his shit about this. Fucker.

"Then you handle it. I'm outta here."

"What? Ave, what're you talking about?"

He was talking about leaving. Holy fuck. He was gonna do it. He was going. "I'm talking about moving out. I'll get my shit out of here by this weekend."

Louis just shut down on him, face going all blank again, perfectly expressionless. "I'll need your half of the rent, then."

Jesus, the man was made of concrete. Not even a twitch, when Avery thought his chest was gonna cave in. "Fine. I'll write you a check."

"Fine." Louis took the towel from Avery's clenched hands and very deliberately dropped it on the floor. "Just let me know if you need any help moving."

With that, Louis turned away from him, leaving Avery standing in the hall staring after him, trying to breathe.

Avery couldn't believe it was that simple. He was leaving. Just like that.

Fuck.

Chapter One

The place was too quiet.

Louis never thought he would even think that, after the way Avery's constant flow of techno music and classical shit drove him crazy, but there it was. His footsteps echoed in the emptiness of the big two-bedroom.

Made him feel like he was lost.

In the two weeks since Ave had left, Louis had worked steady, putting in enough overtime to cover a fricking heart transplant, let alone the shoulder surgery he was about to have. The work kept him away from home, kept the loneliness at bay. Now that he was off for the duration of his surgery and recovery though, he was feeling it. He was missing Ave.

God, he couldn't believe Avery would leave him like that. Just take up and go. Sure, things had been rocky for a bit, with him hurting all the time, the slightest touch making him feel like a grizzly being poked out of hibernation, but he couldn't help it. Wasn't like he wanted to switch jobs, either, but his boss had shafted him, not wanting to pay the comp, shutting down the construction company and saying there was no work. Plenty of work for the fucker in roofing, though, which was the next business the shithead had opened, hiring a bunch of newbies to do piss poor work for no money.

A lawsuit was perfectly reasonable, but Louis wasn't one to air his laundry in court, and he couldn't blame the whole shoulder fiasco on Don, anyway. The injury was old and just kept getting worse, what with him using and abusing the joint hanging sheetrock and drywall, so Louis just kept on keeping on, getting another job and new insurance and taking out a small loan to cover what no one else would.

Stood to reason that he didn't need Ave bitching at him about towels, for fuck's sake, and if Ave could leave him so easily, good riddance to him.

Didn't keep him from being lonely.

Louis sighed, something he couldn't remember ever doing so much of in his whole damned life, and picked a shirt up off the floor, sniffing it. Good enough. He had a whole day between tonight and surgery to recover, so he was going out, having a few beers, and maybe hooking up with someone hot for a kiss and a grope in the back of a bar somewhere. Yeah, that would take his mind off everything.

The shirt looked nice with his cargo pants, and his curly brown hair never reacted well to a comb, so Louis figured that was as good as it was gonna get. He checked his teeth for the remnants of his hamburger helper dinner and headed out. Even with the bad shoulder he had a damned good body from working construction all his life and, despite the dark circles under his eyes, Louis figured he could find someone who liked the look of him well enough.

Hell, the kids he met in bars these days hardly looked at his face, anyway. Horny little fucks.

That's what Avery was when Louis met him. A horny little fuck with a great big hard on and eyes like Napoleon brandy, smooth and amber, but with a spark that took his breath. All Louis could think of back then was sinking his hands into that thick, blond hair and sinking his aching dick into that round, little ass. Too damned bad things went sour.

Too bad Avery never realized that nobody was fucking perfect.

Shaking off the depressing train of thought, Louis hit the street, heading for his favorite watering hole. The Treehouse had good drinks and a tiny dance floor that two guys could go to town on and the music was just what he liked, rough and metallic.

The beer was so cold his teeth hurt from drinking it and the dim, smoky interior of the bar was the perfect place to lose himself. Some kid, who looked to be a heck of a lot younger than Louis' own thirty-eight years, asked him to dance and he did just that, pressing against that tight young body and swaying, letting everything else go.

When it came time to go back to the back and let the kid suck his load right out of him as promised, though? He couldn't do it. Couldn't see anything but Ave's disappointed look. The kid wasn't Ave, and no matter how Louis tried to deny that he wanted Ave back, no one else's lips and tongue would do.

Shit. It was time to go home and sleep it off so he could get ready to have his shoulder rebuilt. He'd do his damnedest to get over Avery.

It was just gonna take time.

***

The surgery went like a dream. Louis spent one night in the hospital before going home with a bucketful of pills and more appointments for physical therapy than any one man should have to put up with. He got his buddy Dave from the crew to drop him off, as he couldn't drive yet, and settled on the couch, drugged to the gills.

Just about the time he dropped off into a light doze the phone rang, making him jump and moan and cradle his left arm. Fuck, that hurt. He couldn't quite figure out how to move, how to untangle his good arm and slide across the couch to grab the handset of the portable, so by the time he was awake the answering machine had clicked on.

"Hey, Lou." God. It was Ave's voice and it made his stomach jolt. "I know we're not really, you know, talking, but I know your surgery was today. I, uh, I hope everything went good. Call me if you need anything."

A long silence cracked over the line.

"Well. Bye."

The machine clicked off as abruptly as it had come on, and Lou stared at it as if by killing it dead with his look he could figure out what the Hell Avery was thinking. It was... well, it was just like Avery to call, just because he was worried, even if they weren't on good terms. Avery did shit like that. Not that Ave was prissy, or girly or anything, towels or not. He was just, well, Louis called it Southern, with a capital S. He asked after people and called to make sure people who had the flu were okay and checked up on ex-lovers when they had surgery because it was the right thing to do. Fuck, that was one of the things Louis loved most about the man, and one of the things that drove him right around the bend.

Pondering calling Ave back just made his head hurt, and that made his stomach all swimmy, so Louis gave up, and heaved his sore self up off the couch, heading for the bathroom, which was damned hard with one arm, before shuffling off to the bed, stripping down and crawling in. He'd think about Avery tomorrow. And the next day and the next, no doubt. Tonight he'd just let the drugs take him, and get some sleep.

***

Avery hung up the phone, staring at it until his brother went by and whacked him on the head, making him yelp.

"Snap out of it, asshole, and go do some laundry."

A dark look was his only reply. He got up, though, and got the laundry basket, picking up all of Justin's dirty socks and stuffing them in. Lord knew he wasn't as anal as Justin made him sound, or as bad as Louis had accused him of being, but he did hate dirty laundry on the floor. Mama's fault, no doubt, though it was a gene Justin didn't seem to inherit.

"You gonna moon about him much longer?"

"Fuck you."

"My my my. You kiss mama with that mouth?"

Putting his feet down very deliberately, Avery headed for the basement, fixin' to do about fifty loads of laundry. Damn Louis anyway. Damn him for making Avery mad enough to move out and for not trying to stop him when he did and for not answering the fucking phone so Ave could stop worrying about him.

Not that he really knew what to worry about. Shit, he didn't even know what the surgery was really all about. He knew Lou had a bad shoulder and that the joint hurt all the time. He even knew that the surgery was supposed to be fairly simple, but that was it. Louis never shared the details, never told him what the doctor said, never told him how it happened. Sometimes living with Louis had been like living with a stranger.

He poured detergent into the running wash water and loaded whites into the machine. Thing was that Louis wasn't a stranger. Ave knew how Louis smelled, what his face looked like when he came, and just how much gravy was enough on his biscuits in the morning. All of that was important stuff, but so was, "Hey I lost my job and oh by the way I'll be in the hospital on day X, you wanna drive me?"

So here he was, living with his baby brother and washing disgusting socks and underwear, wondering how straight guys ever got girls. Surely the women of the world were no more fond of tighty-whities with unidentified stains. Come to that, Avery never understood the whole porn convention of stuffing a guy's briefs in his face. Just didn't make sense.

Neither did him calling Louis. Well, the calling made sense; he wasn't such an asshole that he didn't want to know what was going on with the whole hospital thing, but fuck if the whole longing silence on the message he left made sense. Anyone who could let him go that easy wasn't worth him pining over. Two weeks wasn't very long to get over two years, but maybe he needed to get out there and get some. Not a date, or a new long-term thing, just some hot, rough sex to get him kick-started into the getting over it process.

Avery trudged back up the stairs, trying hard not to run over the what-ifs anymore, but he couldn't help it. They stood out so clearly, those if onlys. Like, what if Louis had just been more open, or what if Louis had been less of a slob? God knew he adored the man's body and he loved Louis' sense of humor, but those little things just added up and the big things like lack of communication tipped the scale toward the bad.

He hit the living room, and the sight of Justin sitting on the couch in a pair of holey sweats, socks strewn on the floor, flipping channels with the remote decided him. He was going out. That was all there was to it.

***

He looked pretty good. Black jeans, a white button up shirt, open at the throat, and his black boots. Avery ran a hand through his hair, making sure it looked uncontrived and checked his rear view one last time. Excellent.

"You going out cruising?"

His hands flexed and Avery grimaced. Justin was coming closer to be strangled in two weeks than Louis ever did in two fucking years.

"Yeah, in fact I am. Don't wait up for me."

"Don't bring some weird guy home."

"Don't worry. I wouldn't want anyone to meet you."

Avery slammed the door behind him, breathing deep of the night air. Fall in South Carolina was cool and crisp, the only time of the year that the humidity eased off enough that you could enjoy how the air felt on your skin. He headed for The Castle, the biggest of the gay bars in town, and the best place for cruising. He liked the music, too, very techno and abstract. He got a drink just because it was polite to throw the bar some money, then hit the floor, bouncing around the edge until he saw someone that looked likely, a freckled redhead with pale, pale skin that looked oddly blue under the light show.

The kid grinned at him and Avery grinned back, moving through the crowd, pushing right into the kid's space and grooving with him. It was good. If he closed his eyes he could almost believe everything was okay. The music throbbed, pushing his hips and his heartbeat faster and faster and Avery let it take him, pretending he was with Louis and not some kid named Ed who was ten years younger than he was and a stranger to boot.

They ended up in the hallway beyond the bathroom, just behind the payphone hanging on the wall, Avery leaning against the hard plaster and Ed on his knees in front, sliding a rubber on Avery and sucking like a Hoover.

Even with his eyes closed he couldn't mistake that for Louis. Louis sucked his cock like it was a feast to be savored, licking and nibbling and loving. Ed sucked him like he was a mountain to climb or an obstacle course to maneuver. Crude, but effective, and soon enough Avery grunted and came, hips snapping hard. Poor Ed got a handjob, because when he squirmed up Avery's body for a kiss, it was all Avery could do not to gag at the latex taste. Ed came all over his hand and it felt like he was cheating on Louis, which pissed him off enough that he just went home, kissing Ed gently and thanking him for a good night, which it damned well wasn't. Still, you had to do what was right and when a man got you off, you made sure he knew he'd made you feel good.

***

A week later Avery caved in and called Louis again, not having heard a damned peep from him, and needing to know that he was okay. The phone rang once and Louis' voice on the other end of the line made his stomach flip over.

"Hello?"

Avery cleared his throat. "Hey. I, uh. Just wanted to check in. You never called me back." Way to go, Ave, he thought. Call, say hi, make an accusation.

"Yeah. I've been sleeping and doing therapy. That's about all the energy I have."

"Oh. But you're okay?"

"Yeah."

They sat there after that, silence stretching between them, and finally Avery gave in. "Right. Well, I was just checking. Bye."

Hanging up before he could say something stupid, Avery wiped his hands on his thighs and went to get a glass of water. At least now he knew Louis was fine.

Just fine.

***

Louis hung up, staring into space for a minute, massaging his bad shoulder with his other hand. Damn Avery anyway for making him jumpy as a cat in a room full of rocking chairs. Just when he'd gotten the soreness out the jerk called and made him tense up again.

The shoulder was healing well. The therapy went easier than he expected, though he had a long road ahead before he could go back to work full-time. Things were going well with that, too, because his new boss had asked him to start doing estimates and pre-job surveys, something he could do fairly easily with one arm and a twink assistant.

In short, he was getting on with his life. If he was a little lonely at night and if he still saw Ave's face when he jerked off? That was the way it worked. Three weeks did not a clean break make, right? Maybe he should try the going out thing again. He could make some major sympathy points with the sling and the pressure to pick up a rebound fuck wouldn't be as high while he was still out of it on the pain and the drugs. Maybe he could find someone to just talk to.

That was the problem with him and Avery. The sex had been so good that Louis tended to ignore that Ave was a neat freak, and a social butterfly, and just a little too perky in the morning. Well, the sex, and Avery's sense of humor, and the way his eyes crinkled at the corners. And there he went again, turning left when he should turn right. Damn it.

He went to Out of Bounds, the gay bookstore where he and Ave had gone and gotten their first free HIV test together. Not because he was looking for Ave, but because that was a great place to strike up a conversation and not end up being cruised. Sure enough, the place was not quite crowded, and there were plenty of singles wandering around chatting and smiling and, though it depressed him rather than cheered him, Louis sucked it up and stayed.

He got two phone numbers and an offer for dinner from a third guy, one he accepted, because the guy was cute, kinda quiet and not demanding at all, and Louis figured he'd be a perfect antidote to Avery.

Yeah. It was time to get on with his life. Starting right then.

Chapter Two

One month and counting since Avery had moved out. Somehow he thought missing Louis should have stopped by now. Or at least gotten less painful. Lord knew he should at least move out of his brother's place and act like he wasn't going to move back in any day. His suitcases were still packed, for fuck's sake.

He'd been out. He'd met people. Or maybe re-met people, because Greenville wasn't small, but it wasn't huge either and the gay community tended to huddle together. So his old friends asked after Louis with the kind of prurient curiosity only a good old Southern queen could have, and the newer kids were happy to see he was single, which was as flattering as it was terrifying.

Avery checked his look one more time. He had a date. Not with one of the little boys who made his head hurt, either, but with an older guy, older than him, at least, maybe in his early forties. His date's name was Gordon and Avery met him at work, giving him an estimate and mock up of an interior garden design for an office. Gordon didn't hire him, but insisted it was because he couldn't take a business associate out for a romantic dinner and Avery was just flattered enough to agree.

Gordon seemed nice. From their short acquaintance he was just the sort of guy Avery wanted to get involved with and a polar opposite of Louis. He was talkative, social, cultured, and his office was neat as a pin. So, despite feeling like he wasn't really up to serious dating just yet, Avery agreed to dinner.

Justin gave him no end of shit for primping like he did, but Avery figured the least he could do was look nice. They were going to Seven Oaks, after all, which was not shabby, and besides, Avery liked dressing up once in awhile, something he couldn't remember doing with Louis in a month of Sundays. He straightened his charcoal gray tie and surveyed himself carefully. Not bad. Not bad at all.

They met outside the restaurant and Gordon smiled and took his elbow, the physical touch making him jolt, with surprise more than anything. God, how long had it been since anyone had touched him casually, without sexual intent, like poor young Ed back at the bar a few weeks ago? The light touch made him realize that it was a long time. Things had been worse with Louis than he thought, if it was that hard to remember a simple arm around the waist, or hand on his back.

"Are you all right?"

The words made him jump, too, spoken next to his ear as they were. Avery smiled at

Gordon, knowing it was more rueful than amused. "Yes. Sorry. I was just lost in thought." Gordon held his chair and he sat, smoothing his pants legs absently.

"Do you like the décor? I find it very old world and charming."

"It's very nice." It was, in fact, very nice, though Avery found it a bit fussy. The menu wasn't fussy at all, though, and that was what mattered. He ordered the flounder and the lobster bisque and the gourmet hush puppies. They chatted about their work, Gordon telling him all about real estate and Avery mostly listening. He wasn't so much bored as out of practice and not at all sure Gordon wanted to hear about landscape design.

Just about the time Avery started to relax and enjoy himself over both the meal and the company, he saw a flash of broad shoulders and curly brown hair at the door of the dining room, making his chest go tight. Fuck it all. Sure enough, it was Louis, walking in with some kid who could barely shave, wearing a pair of khakis and a blazer, looking completely out of place. There were dark circles under Louis' eyes, he'd lost weight, and he wore a sling on his left arm, no doubt to keep pressure off the shoulder.

He still looked good, damn him.

Louis noticed Avery about that time and the Look crossed his face, the one Avery thought of as Holy Shit, but to give Louis credit he didn't run. The man motioned to the jailbait date he had with him and walked right over, nodding at him rather tersely.

"Avery."

"Hello, Louis. How are you?"

"Okay."

Louis just stood there, and Avery sighed, knowing it would be polite to introduce everyone and not really wanting to. "Louis, this is Gordon. Gordon, this is Louis and… I'm sorry, hon. What was your name?"

The kid grinned, totally oblivious to the tension that had sprung up at the table. "I'm Kyle."

"Well, it's nice to meet you, Kyle."

That was as far as he could stretch the polite veneer and Avery let it go at that, feeling bad as Gordon and Kyle stumbled through nice to meet yous, but unable to face the bright curiosity in their eyes or the shuttered disappointment in Louis'. Finally Louis just nodded at him, .

"Nice to see you, Ave."

"Yes. Nice to see you, too."

Just like that it was over, Louis leading Kyle away. Well, that wasn't so bad. Avery could live with that. Really. He could.

"Who was that?"

Shit. Gordon.

"Uh. My ex." Hell, Gordon would hear it sooner or later, if they went out again. "We lived together for a few years."

Gordon smiled at him, blue eyes kind. "Recent ex?"

"A month."

"I'm sorry."

"Don't be." Ave took a deep breath and smiled back, a little too brightly maybe, but real for all that. "Listen, do you mind if we go somewhere else for dessert?"

"Not at all." Gordon's hand was warm where it came to rest on his, not callused like Louis'. "How about my place? I have some leftover cream pie and I can make some coffee."

Was he ready for that? A single glance over at Louis and the adorable Kyle made up his mind for him. Avery took a deep breath. "Sure. I'd like that."

***

Fuck a duck, as his dad would've said. Louis got him and Kyle seated and through the ordering phase without too much trouble, but his mind was racing. Who was that guy? Mr. Distinguished salt and pepper hair and blue eyes Gordon? And why was Louis letting it get to him so bad? After all, he was there with a date, one whom he was ignoring rudely.

"Hey, sorry. My ex."

Kyle shrugged. "Figured. He's hot."

Louis relaxed a little. Kyle was his kinda guy, not all sensitive and crap. "Yeah. But picky, you know? Bitched at me for leaving towels on the floor."

"Oh man, that would drive me nuts."

"Yeah."

Jeez, why did he even bring Kyle to the Seven Oaks, anyway? He could say it was because he was raised that on the first date you took your new guy to a nice place, which was true enough, but it was probably more like Ave was always bugging him to go there and they never got around to it, so subconsciously he picked it. Fine way to start the evening.

His food saved him from further rumination on that and Louis set out to have a good time. Wasn't hard, because Kyle was a good kid, easy to be around, not too talky and nice to look at. Especially eating that custard stuff, licking it off the spoon the way he did. Thank goodness he wasn't dead. After his first disastrous outing to the bar after Avery left, he was beginning to wonder.

Bolstered by his half-mast dick, Louis went so far as to ask the kid back to his place, earning himself a brilliant smile.

"Hey, that would be great. Do you have beer?"

"No, but we can stop and get some on the way home."

The beer had sorta run out and not been replaced, thanks to the pain pills they had him on. It just wasn't good to mix the two. Louis figured it was time to stock the fridge again and this time he could by Schaefer or Nat Light and not worry about whether Ave would want frou-frou microbrew.

"Cool."

His credit card came back and off they went, back to his place. The apartment still showed signs of Avery's design talent, but the floor was strewn with clothes and the sink was full of dishes. Kyle didn't seem to mind; he just popped open a beer and pushed Louis down on the couch and proceeded to suck his tonsils out through his mouth.

Nope. He definitely wasn't dead. His cock went from maybe to oh yeah and Louis did his best to turn off his brain and just let his body have its way. Kyle was a nice kisser, a little rough and careless, but that was youth for you, and Louis could remember being that young and that eager. The old body was doing pretty well, save for the occasional twinge of his shoulder and Louis pulled back far enough to mutter, "Nothing too acrobatic, Kyle."

"Your shoulder ok?" The kid was just petting and panting, hands sliding under his clothes.

"S'fine. Just don't want to hurt."

"Cool. I can do careful."

Damned if Kyle couldn't do careful, in more ways that one. Kid got them both naked, got a condom on him, got them both lubed, and rode him until neither one of them could see, all the while holding onto the back of the couch instead of his shoulders. His free hand stayed on Kyle's hip until the very end, when he grabbed the kid's cock and stroked, watching in fascination as that hot little prick jerked and danced and shot for him.

They didn't shower together, Louis protesting that it was hard enough to get two people in there without a sling and a plastic bag, and that was true enough. He ought to know, he and Ave had squeezed in there enough times, and usually had the bruises to show for it. A hitch of breath and a few tears surprised him, because damn it, Ave was the one who left, not him, and he'd just had mind-blowing sex with a very hot young man. What the fuck did he have to get all fucking maudlin over?

Louis curled up in bed with Kyle, both of them clean and warm.

"I like your soap," Kyle said, and Louis didn't tell him that the lemon piney scent was the one Avery picked out for him.

He just grunted and went to sleep, letting Kyle snuggle up to his back, keeping everything else off it.

***

Gordon had a nice apartment. The lines were clean and modern, the colors chrome and black and gray, and the plants immaculate and healthy. Perfect. It was odd, really, after two years of Louis and a month or more of Justin. Somehow, it gave him hope for his own eventual place. He felt like calling Louis and saying, "See? It can be done."

Not that he would. Ever. Especially not now with Gordon settling him comfortably on the leather couch and going to get him pie and coffee, liberally laced with whiskey. Avery's eyes watered.

"Are you trying to get me tipsy and take advantage of me?"

"Will it work?" Gordon's smile was urbane, smooth, and about as sexy as a block of wood, which was a shame, because he was a pretty one.

"That depends on whether you can loosen up. Are you upset about meeting up with my ex?"

"I admit, it threw me for a loop." That was better, Gordon's smile turning rueful, that molasses and rum voice making the words slide across the space between them. "He's not at all what I would have expected."

Avery fought not to bridle at that. "Really? Why's that?"

"Well, he's very… earthy. Which might be a bad turn of phrase for someone who works in garden design."

"Blue collar, you mean." Sipping his coffee, Avery watched over the rim of his cup as Gordon squirmed.

"Not at all. Simply not as polished as one would expect from someone of your taste and sophistication."

Nice save, he thought. "It was what I liked about him at first. What about you?" Avery asked, changing the subject. "Any exes I need to worry about popping up at dinner?"

"No. I've been a bit too tied to work. I'm willing to explore the possibility, though."

"Of me becoming an ex?" God, what was with him? Here was a man he could converse with and he was pulling out the shears and cutting him to ribbons. "I'm sorry. I'm not usually so rude."

"I imagine seeing him unsettled you."

"Yes." Avery smiled. "I ought to just go."

One of those so smooth hands cupped his cheek. "I wish you would stay. I don't want to push you, but please, don't let him ruin our evening."

Right. Gordon was right. No need to let Louis get to him. From the looks of how Louis and Kyle were deep in flirtation when he left, it certainly hadn't gotten to Louis.

"I'll stay."

"Oh, good."

When Gordon kissed him it was like a work of art, a dance so finely choreographed that Avery found it hard to believe the man was alone that much. Their lips and tongues meshed and twined, Gordon's hands coming up to cradle his head as they stretched out along the couch. Cream pie and coffee and whiskey were there, along with something smooth and soft, something he would come to think of as Gordon. Sophisticated kisses.

They got naked slowly, Gordon much more into foreplay than Louis and, if it lacked something in desperation, their sex made it up in technique. Gordon turned him every which way but loose, practically inside out, invading him with fingers and tongue and finally prick, leaving him wrung out and gasping, a pile of sweaty satiation.

Seemingly just as pleased as he, Gordon kissed him lightly before going out on the tiny balcony attached to the apartment's dining room to have a smoke. The acrid scent of cigarettes accompanied Gordon back inside and they both went right to the shower, finally stumbling to the bed just as their leg muscles started to give out.

The bed was beautiful, a giant mahogany four poster that took up most of the room. It was perfect.

Somehow it made him miss Louis' chipped, green-painted brass monstrosity all the more.

***

Avery woke up warm and horny, rubbing happily against the solid body next to his. God, he'd missed waking up next to Louis, missed the heat and the feel of smooth skin and morning wood. He blinked, a little blurry in the early morning light, and realized he wasn't with Lou. Gordon. That was the guy's name. Avery was with Gordon, in the perfect bedroom.

Sighing, he kissed Gordon's shoulder, trying not to resent the memories. Damn, he was tired of dwelling. Gordon rolled over, smiling sleepily at him, and for a while he forgot, drowning in silk duvet covers and ticklish chest hair and the feel of Gordon's long dick. They fucked long and leisurely again, just like the night before, exchanging kisses that went on forever. They rubbed each other raw with morning stubble and moved together until they came hard.

When Gordon wrinkled his nose and went to have a shower before breakfast, Avery quietly pulled on his clothes and slipped out, leaving Gordon a note saying he had agreed to meet his brother for brunch, which was rude as Hell, but no more so than oh so politely telling him he stank in the morning by running away to scrub him off.

Justin grunted at him when he walked in the door and bitched about tripping over a pair of sneakers in the foyer. Avery ignored it. All he wanted was a steaming plate of eggs and bacon, a shower, and about a ten hour nap. Not necessarily in that order.

Yeah. That first date went really well, didn't it?

***

Louis woke up to Kyle sucking his cock. It was nice, to have his balls cradled gently, his prick pushing into a tight, hot mouth. The kid was okay, if a little sloppy, but sloppy could be fun, so Louis went with it, humping up and feeding it to the kid good, letting Kyle slurp and lick and pull hard on him. In no time at all he was coming, shooting into the rubber Kyle had put on him, slumping on the bed afterward.

"That was cool. I gotta go. Promised to meet the guys for hoops at ten. Is it okay if I grab a pack of pop tarts on the way out?"

Kyle bounced up and rummaged on the floor, coming up with clothes and kissing him hard on the mouth even as he nodded and said, "Sure." He didn't even have time to blink before Kyle left, a cheery, "See ya," trailing behind him.

Shit.

The least the kid could have done was snuggled a little before running out like that.

Avery loved to snuggle.

Louis got up to take a piss and grab something to eat.

Oh, yeah.

That had gone well.

Chapter Three

Two weeks later, Louis was still going out with Kyle. He didn't want to call it dating, because he didn't think that was what it was. Neither he nor Kyle were looking for anything serious and it was mostly dinner and a movie and some serious fucking. The kid had a sweet ass and cheap taste in beer, and that was okay with Louis.

Somehow Kyle ended up staying over a lot and his clothes ended up right on the floor with Louis'. Sooner or later one of them was going to hurt themselves tripping on it, or it was going to do a Calvin and Hobbes thing, where it came to life and ate them, so Louis decided to do some laundry.

Only to find out that he didn't have any detergent or dryer sheets.

Shit. Ave must have taken them with him and was it really that long since he'd done laundry?

Giving up on sorting the clean from the dirty, Louis packed it all in his baskets and hauled it to his car. No way was his little stackable washer and dryer going to handle that, not unless he wanted to be at it all day. He'd take it to the Laundromat and stop at

Winn Dixie or Food Lion and get some Tide
on the way.

Hell, if he was going he might as well take
the grocery list and the cooler. He could buy a
block of dry ice to keep the rest cold until he
got home with it. That would make the whole
sorry trip worthwhile, if he could come home
and make a big old pot of Brunswick stew and
maybe some corn dumplings. Louis wasn't
much of a cook, but Avery's Mama had taught
him how to make stew and dumplings so her
baby boy would have it. He didn't have the
heart to tell her that her baby boy was a much
better cook than he was, so he learned to make
that and a strawberry roll, and she was happy.

Half-hour later, Louis steered his cart
through the grocery store, listening to the front
right wheel squeak, loading up on canned corn
and tomatoes. He turned the corner into the
baking aisle to pick up a jelly roll pan and just
about had a heart attack when he ran right into
the lady who'd taught him how to make the
meal he was shopping for.

"Louis! Hey, darlin'. How are you doing? I
was so afraid I wasn't ever going to see you
again."

Avery's mama was a tall, stately woman
with blonde hair that hid any hint of gray and
the same deep, brandy eyes her son carried off
so well. She wheeled her cart right up beside
his and touched his arm. "I was so upset to
hear that Avery moved out, honey. Especially

right when you were going in to get that surgery done. Are you all right?"

God. Louis looked around, feeling his ears go hot when a little old lady with blue hair muttered and turned her cart around to go back down the row away from them. "Yes, ma'am. I'm fine. I mean," he amended when her face started to cloud, "not fine that Ave is gone, but fine with the shoulder. The doctor says it's healing up nice."

"Oh, good." Esther, for she never allowed him to call her Mrs. Lakewood, patted his arm lightly and surveyed his cart. "You're making Brunswick stew! Does that mean maybe..."

"No ma'am," Louis cut her off. "I have a friend coming for dinner. I hope you don't mind me cooking Avery's dinner for him."

"Well, the boy hardly has a patent, Louis."

"Yes, ma'am."

He felt horrible, being so awkward around her. Louis loved Avery's mama, right from the start. When he first met her he told Ave he didn't know moms smelled nice and wore suits to church and smiled like angels. Avery had just laughed at him, but it was the God's honest truth.

"Well, just because you and Avery broke up doesn't mean you can't come to see me, Louis. You hear?"

Relief made him a little dizzy. She didn't blame him. "I hear. Thank you."

"Oh, honey, you're family to me, no matter what." Esther leaned up and kissed his cheek. "Now, I have to go on, but you come by and see me. Promise?"

"I will. I promise."

They parted ways, she humming, he grinning. At least someone didn't blame it all on him.

***

Brunch with his Mama was a bi-weekly occurrence. While it was always a pleasure, this week it was especially nice because Avery didn't have to take Justin with him. Mama would be disappointed, but Avery liked having a bit of time away from the sib, because living together was going to kill them both.

So Sunday morning he dressed and headed off to the South City Grill for steak and eggs and grits. His mother wasn't hard to spot at all, as she always wore a sunny, sorbet-colored suit for Sunday brunch and a hat. The size and shape of the hat indicated her mood and Avery was surprised to see that she wore her huge, yellow, day at the races hat, which meant she had a bone to pick with him.

"Hey, Mama." Avery bent under the hat to kiss her cheek and she patted his own cheek before they sat and she got down to business.

"Hello, darlin'. Do you want coffee or one of those fancy chai things? I think I'll have coffee." She smiled at the waiter and ordered coffee with cream, waiting while he ordered his chai latte. Then she hit him with it. "So guess who I saw at the Winn Dixie last week? Louis, that's who, and the poor dear looked so tired and worn down, if I do say so myself. Why on earth you thought to leave that sweet man I have no idea. He was always so nice to me."

Avery sighed. "Mama, there were a lot of reasons and you damned well know it, pardon my language."

She just sat and looked at him, waiting, and butter wouldn't melt in her mouth, her expression was so guileless. It didn't fool him for a minute.

"No, Mama. That's it. I'm not talking about Louis anymore."

"But, honey, anyone could see you're unhappy. So is he. Maybe you should call him."

"No."

"But."

"No." Leaning forward, elbows defiantly on the table, Avery looked her straight in the eye. "I'm dating someone, Mama. Someone new. His name is Gordon and he's a real estate broker. He cleans his apartment and makes his bed and he cooks, too. He's perfect."

Tiny frown lines appeared between his Mama's eyes. "Oh, honey. Love doesn't have to be perfect. Please tell me what happened with you and Louis. Maybe if I understand I'll shut up about it like you want me to."

Their drinks arrived, and they ordered food, and Avery decided to just get it over with, especially since Justin wasn't there for the airing of the dirty laundry.

"He never talked to me, Mama."

"Meaning what, exactly?"

"Meaning he never told me anything! I didn't find out he was getting laid off until his last two weeks were almost up. He never talked to me about the surgery. Ever. And he wouldn't pick up his damned towels!"

The napkin to the lips ploy was probably meant to hide Mama's smile, but it did a piss poor job. Her eyes positively danced with it. "Oh, baby. Your daddy hasn't talked to me about the things he thinks he should handle for the thirty-seven years we've been married. Some men just don't."

"Well, then, I must take after you, because I want to talk about everything."

"That's the God's truth." She smiled at him freely this time, digging into the plate of smothered hash browns the waiter set before her. "I tried to make sure you knew it was okay to talk about anything, so some woman wouldn't want to bean you with a skillet, like I've always wanted to do with your daddy. Louis, though, he's deep. Quiet."

"Well, deep and quiet shouldn't be such an issue after two years."

"I suppose that's so. I sure did like him, though. So, when do I get to meet Gordon?"

Panic hit him at the very thought. Gordon and his warm kook of a Mama. Oh, man. "Uh. I don't know that he and I are at the meeting family point, Mama."

She gave him and arch look. "Well, you said he was perfect."

He should have known that would come back to haunt him. "Soon, Mama."

"Good. Now eat your breakfast."

"Yes, ma'am."

***

Sunday morning rolled around too quickly for Louis. He'd been out all night Saturday night, keeping up with Kyle, and his body was damned intent on reminding him that while the kid might only be in his twenties, Louis wasn't anymore.

The phone rang just about the time he thought he might be able to get out of bed without horking like a cat with a fur ball, so Louis sat up and answered it.

"Hello?"

"Hi, Louis."

Well, Hell. It was his mother. "Hi, mom. What's up?" His mother never called unless she needed something, or she wanted him to go to church. Being Sunday, it could go either way.

"I was wondering if you could take me to church. You don't have to stay, Mrs. Lefferts says she can drive me home, but your daddy went out last night and hasn't come back with the car."

Stifling a groan, Louis looked from the clock to the warm body next to him, butt up on top of the covers. Picking her up to go to church meant going all the way to Spartanburg, but Lord knew if he didn't he'd never hear the end of it from her, or from her cult-like Church of Christ buddies.

"Yeah, I'll come and get you. Just give me a half hour."

"Okay, hon. Thanks."

"Sure, mom."

He hung up and heaved himself out of bed, moving his shoulder gently. Therapy would have to wait until after he got back. On the way to the bathroom, he smacked Kyle's ass, laughing when the kid jumped a mile and said, "Whazzat?"

"Get up, kid. We gotta go pick up my mom and take her to church."

"We?"

"Yeah. My shoulder hurts. I'm going to let you drive."

Louis went and did his business, coming back to find the kid dressed and hopping around trying to get his second shoe on, pop tart sticking out of his mouth.

"Geez, Lou, I can't. M'sorry, but I promised my little sister I would take her to youth group."

Louis tried hard not to roll his eyes. Was he ever that frickin' young? "Okay. No prob. I'll go by myself. See you tonight?"

"Maybe? I dunno, I have a lot of work to do for my biology lab tomorrow."

College kids, Louis thought. Argh.

"Okay, whatever. Get your ass out of here. I'll see you whenever."

"Cool." The kid pecked a sugary kiss on his lips and was off and running, leaving Louis muttering about schedules, cursing when he tripped over one of Kyle's many pairs of spare sneakers. The least the kid could do was pick the damned things up and tell him ahead of time when he had plans.

Fuck. He was starting to sound like Ave.

That was a damned scary thought.

***

"So how was brunch with your mother?"

Avery was eating dinner with Gordon, having arrived at Gordon' apartment to an exquisitely set table and immaculate meal of lamb with mint sauce and roasted potatoes. The wine complimented everything and there was crème caramel for dessert. It was rather disconcerting.

"Good. She wants to meet you."

"Really? How entertaining! I doubt we know each other well enough yet to be meeting families, though."

Ears hot, Avery nodded. "That's what I told her."

"Excellent. You know, that's one thing I like about you, Avery. We think so much alike."

"Yeah."

Increasingly restless, Avery pushed his asparagus around on his plate. The meeting with his Mama had unsettled him, made him think too much. That, added to Gordon's smug acceptance of their casual dating status made him need to move, maybe walk, or dance. He hadn't been dancing since the night out with the redhead.

"We should go clubbing."

"Beg pardon?"

Gordon's surprise might have been comical if he wasn't so edgy. Instead, it brought out the pure devil in him. "We should go out next weekend. Go to the club. They're having fetish night next week. I could go as your slave."

Oh, that made him feel better, that little, perplexed frown, which was just terrible of him, but bless Gordon's heart, he just brought out the worst in Ave sometimes.

"I doubt that would be a good idea. What if someone from work saw, Avery? I depend on my image."

"Of course you do, Gordon. I was only teasing."

"Oh. Of course."

God, sometimes he missed Lou's offbeat sense of humor. Much as he'd bitched about it cropping up at the oddest times, when he said something like he'd just said to Gordon, Lou would grab him and haul him off to the nearest adult bookstore to buy whips and chains.

Gordon didn't have much of a sense of humor.

The restlessness stayed with him well after dinner, when they sat on the sofa and watched a movie. The only thing Avery could do to relieve it was to scoot up next to Gordon and kiss him, sliding his hands over the smooth silk of Gordon's shirt to pull the man close.

Kissing him back, Gordon put an arm around him, pulling him up tight, and Avery let the touch ease him, let the melding of lips and tongues and skin take away the thoughts swimming in his head until all he knew was heat and sweat and the feel of his orgasm shooting up his spine.

***

Louis gripped Kyle's narrow hips and thrust hard, pushing into the kid's tight, hot ass over and over. The kid was on his knees on the bed, pushing back at Louis and just begging for it with his whole body. Louis used Kyle to wipe out the entire day spent ferrying his mom back and forth to church, listening to her whine about his dad, and him, and every other damned thing in the world.

"Lou. Yeah. Please."

Tilting Kyle up and his own hips just the right way, Louis pegged the kid's gland, making Kyle moan and arch and pant for breath. When it was all about sex and need and spunk, he could forget about all of the other shit, just let it go. Louis loved to fuck, loved the smells and sounds and the feel of someone shaking beneath him. He found Kyle's dick with his hand, pulling hard at it, watching the kid's back muscles ripple, nuzzling at the sweat-dark curls on the back of Kyle's neck.

Yeah, when he fucked he forgot, just went with it and felt good, and he felt good right then, hips snapping as Kyle cried out and shot over his hand, ass clamping down hard on him, pulling his come out of him, making him shout.

The problem came after, when Kyle rolled over and started snoring and Louis was left with his thoughts.

His mom, his dad, and what the Hell he was going to do with his life all sorta crowded in, making him a little crazy. Louis tried not to dwell on things, tried not to be all touchy feely and needy, but sometimes a man just had to look at the direction he was taking and wonder. So Louis wondered and tried to get to sleep, and tossed and turned.

Sometime around one in the morning, Louis wondered what Avery was doing right then and he went to sleep with brown eyes and a dimpled smile heavy on his mind.

***

God, was it New Years already? Fuck. Thanksgiving had been spent with the family, Christmas Eve with Gordon at some fancy party, and Christmas dinner with his mama and daddy and Justin, so Avery really hadn't had time to miss Lou too much.

But New Years. Well, damn. That was always a time for couples, at least to Avery. It was telling that Gordon had invited him to go to another dress up party and Avery had made excuses instead of dry-cleaning his tux.

He watched Dick Clark and ate Lil' Smokies and thought about Louis and Gordon and got maudlin and drank too damned much beer. New Years Eve turned out to be the longest night in a string of long nights and Avery wondered how he had managed to mess things up so bad that he didn't know how to fix them.

***

Louis woke up on New Year's Day with a terrible headache and a nasty taste in his mouth. Fuck, he'd gone out with Kyle and gotten slaughtered. Just drank until the whole night was a blur.

He remembered kissing Kyle at midnight, remembered how wrong it tasted and felt. Remembered giving the kid a handjob because Louis was too damned drunk to get it up and how he'd felt like shit for being glad about it.

Last year New Years had been all about champagne punch and the longest game of Monopoly in history and slow, deep kisses that led to Avery hopping on and riding him until they both fell over from exhaustion. The next day they'd watched football and eaten ham and black-eyed peas.

This year? He didn't even want to get out of bed, but the thought of ham and beans made him, running for the bathroom with his hands over his mouth.

It was amazing how things could change on you.

Chapter Four

Flipping through one of Gordon's Southern Living magazines made Avery contemplate his circumstances. He was thirty-two years old. His job was great, but the firm he worked for had little or no room for advancement and just as little room for real creativity. There was only so much a guy could do with offices and public buildings as far as gardens went.

Maybe it was time to think about something else. Not a different profession, by any means, but a different job. Avery had a little money saved. Maybe he should think about starting his own business. He could go to Greenville Tech, take a few basic accounting courses, start doing private design, maybe by spring, when it would do him the most good. Sure, the money wasn't as easy as corporate one offs, but it would be a lot more fun and he would have all the room in the world to stretch his creative muscles.

Or maybe he was just watching too much Trading Spaces on TV.

"Whatever it is, it must be deep."

"Huh?" Avery guiltily removed his feet from Gordon's sofa and sat up.

"You were so deep in thought you didn't even hear me. I asked if you wanted some iced tea."

"Oh, that would be great."

Gordon left, only to come back with tea and a dizzying array of sweets and little sandwiches. The man was inhuman. "So what was so engrossing?"

"Oh, I was just thinking of going into business for myself."

He dropped it casually, but watched carefully for Gordon's reaction. It ran along the lines of, "Wonderful. Let me know if you need office space. We have some great properties right now."

"Sure. I'll do that." Eating up, Avery brushed the crumbs off his knees carefully into his cupped palm and threw them away before standing and kissing Gordon lightly. "I need to get going. I'll see you later, okay?"

Poor Gordon looked perplexed, but smiled and nodded. "All right."

Avery fled. Once out of Gordon's building he headed directly for Greenville Tech, picking up a brochure on continuing education. They had just what he needed, small business accounting and tax classes. Signing up was a snap and Avery couldn't believe how easily he'd made the decision to at least try. Usually he obsessed about things to the point of pain. Doing something, anything, felt good, and

Avery went back to his brother's place with a smile on his face.

***

"Here's that catalog you wanted, Louis."

"Thanks."

The great thing about dating a college student was when your boss suggested you take some business classes at the local tech college, the kid could get all the paperwork for you and help you figure out how in Hell to fill it all out.

Louis had never gone to college. Ave had, which was kinda cool as far as Louis was concerned, just like Kyle going was a neat thing, but it wasn't something he ever thought to do himself. Not that a few business classes at the adult ed thing was going to college, but school was so not his bag. Still, if it made him better money, which it would with his appraisal work, he'd go for it.

"So how do I fill out all this crap, Kyle?"

"Oh, here."

Half- hour later, Louis had completed paperwork and a snarly disposition. "How in Hell do you people manage to get all this shit done at eighteen?"

Kyle grinned at him. "Parents. And by time you're twenty-one? You learn to do it yourself."

"So you say. Fuck this. Let's have supper."

"Cool! Can we go have wings and pizza?"

"Yeah, whatever you want."

"Cool." Kyle kissed him full on the mouth and off they went to dinner at Barley's Taproom and Pizzeria.

About fifty of Kyle's closest friends were there, or so it seemed, and after the first fifteen minutes or so, Louis started feeling mighty uncomfortable. Looked like they all knew Kyle was "that way", as the Southern euphemism went, so none of them took exception to Kyle sitting a bit too close, okay practically on top of him, but it made Louis feel both old and prudish, because he wanted to push the kid away and tell him to behave.

Instead he spent a miserable evening being scrutinized and flirted with, and Louis went home overfed and out of sorts, and determined to take that second look at his life as soon as possible.

***

Bowling with his dad was a monthly date, sometimes bi-weekly, and though Avery had never felt less like going, it was one he couldn't duck out of. His dad would be disappointed and his mama would never let him live it down. So Avery got his ball and his shoes (both gifts from his dad, who swore he'd get invited to join the league some day) and went, giving Justin a dirty look for good

measure when his brother laughed about him
bonding with the old man over the most boring
sport in history.

The alley was practically empty, only old
man Borges taking up a lane, fat cigar
clenched between his teeth. Avery's father was
there, wearing his ugly, plaid pants and a stoic
look that told Avery he was late.

"Sorry, Dad. Justin was giving me a hard
time."

His father just shook his head and said,
"You boys," and indicated that he was
supposed to keep score.

Avery grinned, shaking his own head in
return. His mama was right. His dad was one
of the most uncommunicative people on earth.
Maybe it was like they said about girls
choosing guys like their dads. As a gay man,
maybe he was unconsciously looking for the
same kind of guy that influenced his whole
childhood and thus sabotaging himself by
thinking he needed something different.

Or maybe that kind of psychobabble was, as
his dad would say, a bunch of hoohaw.

"So how is your brother? Don't see him
much."

Avery almost dropped the bowling ball on
his foot when his dad's voice broke through
his thoughts. Shit.

"Uh. He's fine. Mostly. I try to stay away
from him."

"Yeah? Hear you're living with him. Kinda hard that way."

His dad let loose, bowling a strike right off, which pretty much told Ave what kind of night it was going to be.

"Yeah. Well, I try to come in and out quietly."

A loud snort was his reply and he marked down his dad's score before moving to toss his own ball. If he had the inclination, Avery could probably be pretty good at it, but bowling was always just a hobby he'd taken up to spend time with the old man.

"So when are you and Louis getting back together?"

Goddamn it. Gutter ball. Avery gave his dad the greasy fish eye. "You did that on purpose."

"Did not. Just asking."

"Well, I'm sure you talked to mom, so you know we aren't."

"Uh huh." The funny tiptoe dance and back leg crossover his dad performed could have been in a Disney movie ballet. "Shame. I liked that boy."

"I know, dad."

Of course his dad had liked Louis. They could sit for hours on Thanksgiving Day and watch ballgames and never grunt more than three words at each other. If nothing else, Louis was perfect for his dad.

"Well. Ain't none of my business. You gonna go?"

Avery sighed, nodded, and put his mind to kicking his dad's butt, just to prove to the old man that he could. And to prove to himself that he wasn't letting the whole thing with Louis get him down anymore.

***

"So where's Avery these days?"

"Huh?" Louis knew damned well what Joe had asked, but it still hit him kinda out of the blue.

"We just haven't seen you bring him around since before Christmas

That was because Avery wasn't around to be brought around, but Louis bit that bitter thought back, swallowing it right down. "We broke up."

"Whoa. Man, I'm sorry."

"Yeah."

Poor Joe, he had that look people get when someone tells you they're getting a divorce, or their dog just died. That sympathetic yet really uncomfortable look. Louis didn't say much after that, just sipped his beer, and Joe eventually moved off to sit with someone else.

Good old Joe. Louis could see the word spread like wildfire through his friends and acquaintances at the bar, could see the looks they gave him and the way they whispered to

each other. Hell, he could even understand it.
He'd been on the other side of that. Poor so
and so, they'd say, broke up with his
boyfriend/girlfriend/whatever. Poor, poor so
and so.

He fucking hated it.

***

The first night of class was a nerve-
wracking thing for Louis. He'd never done it
before, and figured he'd be the oldest one in
the class and the dumbest one besides. He
found the classroom no problem and, feeling
horribly like he was back in fucking high
school, settled at the back of the room, trying
to fade into the woodwork.

That gave him a great view of the door and
Louis almost fell over when he saw Avery
walk in. Jesus. What was Ave doing there?
Avery saw him, too, Louis saw it in the
widening of Avery's eyes and the stutter in his
step, but they didn't have time to talk, as the
instructor showed up right about then, and they
were off on three hours of syllabus looking and
an overview of small business accounting.

Louis took notes and carefully made little
charts and wrote down the name of the book
he was supposed to buy, but all the while his
mind spent half its energy on Avery. He
looked, well, tired. Good, but tired. They were
pretty much well matched that way; he still

saw dark circles under his own eyes when he looked in the mirror. That was to be expected, though, with his therapy just ending and him starting back at work full time. He wondered what Ave's excuse was.

The last five minutes of class dragged on and on, and Louis shuffled his papers and kicked his bag. Should he try to catch Ave and say hi? It would be damned impolite not to and, while he was a heck of a lot less concerned about the social niceties than Ave, he still cared about the man. He would at least do that much.

Avery was waiting for him outside the door when he walked out, giving him a nervous half smile, like should I or not? Louis' chest got tight. Damn it, when was he gonna get over it? When was it going to stop feeling like his legs were being cut right out from under him?

"Hey, Ave."

"Hi, Louis. How are you?"

"Okay."

Avery indicated his arm. "The sling is gone."

"Yeah. Two days ago. Still doing therapy. So what are you doing here?"

It came out so abrupt that he winced and Avery lost the smile. "Taking a class."

Slow as molasses in wintertime, that answer, and dripping with sarcasm besides. Vintage Ave. "I meant why? I mean, what for?"

"I'm thinking of going into business for myself."

"Yeah?" Surprised, Louis mulled that over for a moment. "Like, competing with your job now? Or doing something else?"

"Going into private sector work. Home gardens, curb appeal for people's houses, that sort of thing. I'm tired of the corporate bull."

Hell, he'd never thought Avery might be unhappy at his job. As far as he knew, Ave loved the schmoozing and suits and dinner parties that came with designing for the Chamber of Commerce set.

"That's great, Ave. You're really good at what you do."

"Thanks." A pleased, almost shy smile came his way, making him blink as his heart speeded up. Damn, but Ave still got to him with those sherry eyes and that light up the sky grin.

"What about you?"

"Huh?" He floundered, shaking off the goofy feeling. "Oh. I'm going into more of the appraisal side of the business and the new boss wants me to take some classes."

"That's great! So you won't be hurting yourself anymore, right? I mean, not like you were deliberately before, but this is less physical?"

"Yeah." Louis shrugged. "I'll be a crew chief. Plans and shit."

"Fantastic." Ave's pleasure was so tangible and infectious that Louis found himself smiling as well. "Well, I ought to go. I have a dinner thing."

"Oh." Up, down. Up, down. Louis figured he'd need Prozac before much longer. "Okay. Are you still seeing that guy, what was his name?"

"Gordon." Cheeks pink, Avery nodded. "Yes. He's, well, he's very neat and he cooks gourmet."

"Well, whooptie-doo."

"Lou."

Louis sighed. They couldn't even talk for five minutes without Avery getting that tone. "Sorry."

"So what about you? Still robbing the cradle?"

Two could play that game. "Yeah. He doesn't bitch about my towels and he sucks like nobody's business. There's advantages to youth."

"Good for you." Ave was back to being tight and polite, smile completely gone and shoulders stiff. "I need to go. I guess I'll see you Thursday."

"Sure. In class."

"Yeah."

One last, unreadable look and Avery left, walking away and leaving Louis standing there feeling like he'd been hit by a truck.

Nothing ever went the way you expected it to. Ever.

***

"So how was class?"

"Hmm?" Avery looked up from his menu, meeting Gordon's eyes, which were blue and not green and somehow looked odd because they weren't Louis'. "It went okay. How was your day?"

"Oh, I sold a wonderful property just off the golf course."

Right about then Avery stopped listening, even though Gordon kept on talking. It wasn't fair, he knew, as he'd always said he wanted someone talkative, but Avery had little to no interest in real estate and he found himself tuning Gordon out a lot. It didn't seem to matter to Gordon, who just seemed to like to have someone to talk at, which Avery supposed was better than talking to himself.

Dinner went by slowly, because Avery wanted it to be over, and finally Gordon got a clue, touching his hand lightly.

"Are you all right?"

"I'm just tired. I think I should just go home tonight."

"Oh." Surprise and disappointment flashed in Gordon's eyes, but the man was too polite to complain. "Of course. Your first day at school on top of work. You must be tired."

"I am." Smiling, Avery patted Gordon's hand back. The man was nothing if not understanding and Avery felt bad for his occasional uncharitable thought. "I promise I'll make it up to you this weekend. I'll bring the champagne and orange juice, okay?"

"Oh, that sounds nice." Gordon smiled back, this one reaching his eyes, and they went their separate ways after they paid the check.

Avery was still reeling from seeing Louis, and from knowing that Lou was still dating that floppy-haired child he'd seen at the Seven Oaks. He was still dating Gordon, wasn't he? So it stood to reason that Louis might be on the same track.

It still hurt.

He got home to an empty apartment and a note from his brother that Justin would be out all night, nudge wink, which was a relief. Skirting the piles of detritus, Avery went straight to the shower, stripping off and turning the water up as hot as he could stand it. The steam felt good, opening him up, loosening tight muscles, and just for a minute Avery closed his eyes and let himself think of Louis, of green eyes and curly hair hanging in wet hanks and of that hot mouth on him. He thought of Louis' body, hard and tight and square, and of Louis' cock, big and red and so good in his hands and mouth.

When he came, he let the shower wash away the tears as easily as it did his spunk.

***

"Checkmate."

"Hmm?"

"Really, Avery, I felt like I was playing myself that last game. Where were you?" Gordon's expression was all concern, all but the eyes snapping with irritation.

"I'm sorry, Gordon. I probably wasn't up to chess tonight. I should have said so."

He wasn't really up to chess most of the time; while he was proficient at it, he'd never really developed a taste for it, preferring more social games like Monopoly or Scrabble. He had a feeling Gordon thought those games were bourgeois.

With Lou it had been Chinese checkers, marathon sessions on holidays like New Year's Eve where they would each play three colors and do their best to block the other off. Or Scrabble. Or pinochle, played four handed with Carl and Linda, Carl being from Lou's work. They had a cute little bungalow with a sunken living room that they set card tables up in and a cockatoo that bit the shit out of his ear every time he went over.

Avery never saw them anymore, since the break-up.

"I said, should I put the board away then?"

Avery snapped back to Gordon, the impatience in that butterscotch voice making him wince. "Sure. Why don't we just have a glass of wine and watch that movie you got?"

"Certainly. If you think you might pay attention."

"Don't be snide." No way was he going to stand for that. Not after three games of chess.

"I'm sorry, love. I'll get the wine."

Shoulders and back stiff, Gordon went to the kitchen and Avery rolled his eyes. Sometimes it would be nice if Gordon was a little less communicative, at least about his pouts.

Of course, maybe that was just because he'd finally gotten used to Lou.

***

"Louis! Come on in!"

Linda was such a sweet lady, always welcoming him with open arms. Louis handed her the bottle of wine he'd brought and the flowers he'd gotten her, too, making her husband Carl snort.

"Good thing I know you're queer."

"Carl!"

Louis just laughed. "It's okay, Linda. We all know it's true. Hey, Carl."

"Hey, Lou."

They shook hands, and Louis was glad they had asked him over. He hadn't been out to see any of their friends since he and Avery broke up, and he found it was nice to get out with someone who wasn't half his age.

"I hope you don't mind, Louis, but I invited a nice young man from church to be our fourth."

Oh, God. Linda was trying to set him up, he'd bet anything on it. No wonder they hadn't asked after Avery. Louis just nodded and smiled, all of his pleasure in the evening draining away. One way or another, something always conspired to make sure he was never gonna get over this shit with Ave. And it was getting old.

Chapter Five

School was going okay, which kinda surprised him, because Louis didn't think he would like it. The whole business end of business was interesting, which wasn't to say he was gonna put on a suit anytime soon, but he figured he could hack it.

His first test came back with an A and his textbook was getting read and if seeing Avery two nights a week was agonizing, he thought he hid it well.

"It's really cool to have someone to do homework with, huh?"

Louis winced. He'd forgotten Kyle was there. While Kyle thought it was great for them to study together, Louis found it hard. Kyle didn't chatter incessantly, but he did have a bouncy leg and a tapping pencil that set Louis' teeth on edge, and he found it hard not to snap about the difference between Western Civ to a twenty-one year old kid, and business math to an almost forty year old.

"Yeah, cool."

Kyle chewed the end of the pencil, reading down the page a bit more before looking up at him again. "Are you pissed off at me, Lou?"

"Huh?" Okay, maybe he wasn't hiding things as well as he thought.

"You've been majorly tense and really grumpy. I mean if I did something…"

"No. Hey, no. Really." Louis put his own pen down and stood, stretching until his back and shoulder popped like a champagne cork. "Come on, let's take this away from the books; it's math making me grumpy."

The kid grinned at him and bounced up, too. "I'll get us a couple of beers."

"Oh, yeah." He grinned back, heading for the couch. Kyle wasn't much of a snuggler, but the couch would be better than the crowded kitchen table one way or the other. They sat and sipped for a while, neither of them saying much, and Lou wondered how Avery had stood him as long as he did, really, being as talky as he was and Louis as closed-mouthed as a clam.

"Anyway, I'm not mad at you," Louis said, at length. "I'm just… tired. School is hard work for me."

"It is for me, too. I mean, I know you think I'm a young idiot, but I got plans, you know? School is important."

"Oh." Was he really that fucking condescending? Maybe he was, though he hated to think it. "I don't mean to sound that way, Kyle."

Kyle nodded. "I know. You're a good guy, Lou, but you get really wrapped up in your own shit, you know?"

"Yeah. Yeah, I guess I do." He did, probably for the first time fully understanding what Ave meant when he always said Louis was a closed-mouthed bastard who thought only of himself. Well, Ave never said it that way, but there it was. That didn't mean he had to get all in touch with his feminine side, but maybe he could learn a few new tricks, like seeing both sides of the problem.

"So I'll try not to snap at you if you don't drum your pencil on the table?"

Laughing, Kyle leaned in and kissed him. "I didn't know it bugged you. You got a deal."

Enjoying the resilient warmth of Kyle's firm young body, Louis started petting. To heck with the homework. "Cool."

***

Panting, Avery collapsed on Gordon's beautiful bed and lay there, sweat drying on his body, the feel of Gordon's long prick still making his ass twinge. The man fucked like a well-oiled machine and tonight that was exactly what he'd needed.

"Mmm. Thank you."

Gordon laughed, air puffing against his neck. "No, no. Thank you."

Gordon had a lovely voice at the worst of times. At times like this, it was downright inspiring. Avery turned carefully, arms coming up, and Gordon came right into them, fitting easily against him.

"Are you ready to tell me what's wrong?"

Avery stifled a sigh. Some days it was wonderful to have someone who liked to talk. Some days he wished Gordon would just leave it alone. Guess which this one is, he thought. Didn't anyone just snuggle anymore?

"It's really nothing I can put a name to. I think I'm just at that point where everything needs to be examined and I would rather bury my head in the sand."

"Are you examining me as well?"

"I just did, didn't I?" Oh, that was vintage Louis and it made him want to laugh as much as it put a lump in Avery's throat. Would it never end?

"You know what I mean." Gordon's tone was chiding, a gentle rebuke that only someone born and raised in the South could manage, drawing the words out just so.

"Yes. I know what you mean. I'm sorry if I seem to be…"

"Using me?"

Oh, dear. "Well, if that's how it seems, then yes. I'm sorry for it."

"Not at all." Gordon's hands were warm where they rested on his hip, his lower back. "Neither of us expects anything, or at least I

don't. I hope you don't. It's perfectly obvious
that you're still in love with your ex, and
frankly Avery, while I like you a great deal,
and desire you even more, I am not the
commitment type. You'll notice me not asking
you to move in. I like my life as it is."

That should have relieved him. Instead, the
bald statement of intent unsettled him, made
him uncomfortable as Hell. "Yeah. I can see
that."

"Now you're upset."

"No. Just... a little lost, I guess." Avery
wanted to get up and go, but that would be
rude as anything and prove Gordon right
besides. Idly, he wondered what he would tell
his Mama when she poked him again about
meeting his new man.

"Well, it's not as though I want to kick you
out, Avery. I just want you to know how I
feel."

Right. It was good to know, wasn't it? He
always said he wished Louis would let him
know where he stood. Gordon was more than
happy to do that.

"Perfect."

***

The next day, Avery stumbled through two
meetings with new clients, a consultation with
a small business financial advisor and lunch
with his boss, who asked him outright when he

was going to quit, which made him smile. The old man didn't pull any punches and Avery thoroughly enjoyed the debate on the stability of the home design market.

His mind was on other things, though, namely Louis and what Gordon had said about Avery still being in love with him. Was it true? Most likely. Did that help him any? Probably not.

It had been five and a half months. Surely he should be getting over it by now. Maybe he just didn't want to, or maybe he just couldn't. Something his Mama said to him once kept repeating in his head over and over. Love doesn't have to be perfect, baby, she'd said, and maybe it wasn't Louis that drove them apart. Maybe it was Avery's expectations. Lord knew Gordon should be the perfect man for him and look at what was going on there. Perfection certainly didn't equal love on that front.

For the first time since classes started, Avery found himself looking forward to seeing Louis, rather than dreading it. If nothing else, maybe they could talk, be civil. Avery missed that.

Class finally rolled around and he spotted Louis coming in, looking edible in faded jeans and work boots and a sweater Avery remembered throwing in the trash once, which had pissed Louis off to no end, though a blowjob had gone a long way to making the man feel better about having to hand wash it to get the ketchup stain off it. The memory made him smile widely and when Louis caught his eye, Avery got a surprised look. Yeah. Let Louis chew on that grin for a while.

After class he caught Louis on the way out the door, making a mental note not to get snooty like he had last time they'd talked. Just keep it light.

"Hey, Lou."

"Ave." Louis looked at once cautious and pleased

"How did you do on the quiz?"

"I got an A."

"Way to go!" He was genuinely pleased that Louis seemed to be doing well in class. He always thought Lou had more going on than the man gave himself credit for.

"Yeah. You?"

"I did okay. Got an A minus."

One dark eyebrow went up in a way that meant Louis was surprised, but too polite to say so. For some reason it made him grin rather than pissing him off.

"So, listen, I was wondering. Thursday, maybe, I was thinking we could go to coffee after class."

Both eyebrows shot up then and Avery bit his lip to keep from laughing. It was hard, because the chuckles kept trying to bubble up, anyway.

"You don't have anything planned with what'shisname?"

"Not a thing." No way was he going to rise to the bait. Gordon wasn't even a consideration. That was as plain as the nose on his face. "I thought we could just get together and talk."

"Oh." The wheels were turning, Avery could see that. Louis mulled it over for a full minute. Avery refused to give in to the urge to shift from foot to foot. "Yeah, okay, Ave. Sure."

Relieved, Avery bounced on his toes, smiling, and Louis blinked at him.

"Cool. I'll see you after class then."

"Yeah. See you then."

It wasn't perfect, because Lou still looked stiff and unsure and off balance. They would dance around each other and probably poke each other with sharp sticks of memory and get pissy and have to deal, but to Avery it was worth it to have Louis in his life one way or another, even if it was just as a friend. No, it wasn't perfect, but it was a start.

***

Louis surprised himself by getting home without driving into anything. Who in Hell knew Ave would do something like that, asking him out for coffee? Shit, he figured after their last little talk it was all over, that Avery would ride off into the sunset with his perfect new man who cooked and cleaned and Louis wouldn't hear from him again.

He had to clamp down really hard on the silly exhilaration he felt. God, his cheeks were all red and he felt like an idiot, but he had a date with Ave. For coffee. Right, just coffee. Just a friendly thing. He had to remember that.

The phone rang as he passed it, startling the Hell out of him, making him yelp. Louis picked it up, answering with a distracted, "Hello?"

"Louis? Honey?" It was his mother, and she sounded positively panicked.

"Yeah, mom? What's up?"

"Oh, honey, I'm so glad I got you, finally. Your daddy's had an accident, he ran a red light. He's in the hospital and I can't get the doctor to tell me what's happening and I think he's hurt. Honey, can you..."

"Yeah, mom. I'll be right there. Just tell me where you are."

"We're at Mary Black, Lou. On Skylyn. You know where I mean?"

"Yeah. See you soon."

Louis hung up and got his keys, wallet, and jacket back out and headed out to make the forty-five minute drive to Spartanburg. Damn his daddy anyway, but the man always did have the worst timing in the world.

***

Three days later it occurred to Louis that he'd not only missed class, he'd missed his date with Ave, too. Fuck a duck.

His dad was all busted up, had a broken hip and a broken knee, and Louis had spent three long days back and forth at the hospital and the rehab transitional center, where his daddy was now. His mom finally got a hold of some of her church people after Louis' daddy started cussing him and Louis told her he was going to break more than knees and hips, so she had a ride back and forth now and plenty of squash casserole and ham and biscuits to keep her fat and happy. Louis just wanted to go home.

He finally did on Friday, coming home to an empty apartment, as he'd told Kyle not to expect him and that he'd call. Call. Shit, he had to call Avery, but he didn't have Justin's phone number. He did have Avery's Mama's number, though, and before he went and collapsed he dialed her up.

"Hello?"

"Hey, Esther. It's Louis."

"Louis, darlin'! How are you?"

"Not so good, ma'am. My daddy had a bit of an accident."

"Oh, dear. How's your mother?"

"She's doing all right. Look, do you have Justin's number? I was supposed to see Avery yesterday and I clean forgot, what with the hospital and all."

"You were going to see Avery?" Esther sounded right pleased with the prospect. "Well of course I do, honey. They're both my sons, aren't they?"

She always made him blush over something, even when she couldn't see him. "Yes, ma'am."

"Now, I have Avery's new cell phone number somewhere. Why don't I just give you that?"

"That'd be fine." He waited while she found it and rattled it off, dutifully writing it down. "Thanks, Esther."

"Not a problem. When you and Avery get it all settled, y'all come over for dinner sometime, okay?"

Too tired to argue that it wasn't like that. Louis just said, "Sure. Thank you, Esther."

"You take care, now, hon."

"Yes, ma'am."

He had a feeling the next call was going to be much harder.

***

Avery's cell rang just as he was about to head out the door for dinner with Gordon. Sighing, Avery answered, figuring it was his mother and not even looking at the number.

"'Lo?"

"Avery? Hey. I… it's Lou."

Lou. Louis, who hadn't shown up to class yesterday and subsequently not made their coffee date. Avery bit back the snap that wanted to come out and took a deep breath.

"Hey, Louis. What's up?"

"I hope you don't mind, but I called your Mama for your new number. I'm sorry about last night, Ave. My dad's in the hospital, He broke his hip."

"Oh, Lord, Lou. Is he gonna be okay?" All of the stiff anger he'd carried around all day was gone, concern taking its place.

"He's too mean to die." Lou sounded tired, voice just slurring around the edges.

"How's your mama? You need anything?"

"No, I. Well, she's fine and I'm just tired. I do need something, though."

"Yeah? What can I do?"

"Give me another chance? Supper tomorrow?"

It was so unlike Lou to ask, or to make that kind of an effort to explain, and it made Avery's heart race. For God's sake, it was just supper.

"You bet. Where?"

"Why don't you meet me at Fuddrucker's and we'll have burgers."

Avery wondered if Louis was feeling the same crushing sense of relief he was. "Sure. About five?"

"That'd be great."

"Cool. I'll see you then."

"Yeah. Bye, Ave. And thanks."

They hung up and Avery found himself standing in his doorway, grinning like an idiot. Louis hadn't meant to miss their date. Louis had called him, not made him wonder and stew and worry. Louis had asked *him* for a rain check and made the next move.

He might just fall over from the shock.

Shit. Gordon. Avery locked up and hopped in the car, heading out to dinner. He'd have to stop bouncing if he didn't want Gordon to ask what was going on and he found that he didn't. It was too good to share yet, and while Gordon had been really decent about his thing with Louis, it was impolite to wave it in someone's face.

Still, he couldn't believe it. Louis had called him.

Hot damn.

***

"Goddamn it, Louis, if I wanted your help I would ask for it. I can do this my own damned self."

Louis sighed, looking at his dad try to struggle up out of the chair using the walker the therapy place had sent home with him. From the corner his mom watched, wringing her hands, but not offering one bit of help. Of course, he could kinda understand that, the way his dad was acting about him trying to put one hand under his dad's elbow to steady the man while he teetered.

He never liked to accept help either, did he? He'd growl at anyone who thought he wasn't capable and snarl at anyone who tried to act like his shoulder injury made him less able. It was scary, sometimes, how much he was like his dad, because Louis didn't want to end up a bitter old bastard who drank too much and wrecked his life as often as he did his cars.

One way or the other, the old man didn't want his help, so Louis went to his mom instead, quietly offering to go get her groceries and earning himself a tremulous smile. To Hell with the old man, he thought. And to Hell with following in his father's footsteps. He could learn to let people help him. And he would even if it killed him.

Chapter Six

Louis straightened his collar for what must be the hundredth time, trying not to stare out the window of the burger place to see if Ave was pulling into the lot. Poor Kyle had been a little disappointed they weren't doing something together, but the kid was deceptively intuitive and let it drop when Louis got defensive.

Not that there was anything to get defensive about. It was just a burger with an old friend. That was it. Not a date, not a reconciliation, not anything like that. Hell, Louis wasn't sure he even wanted to reconcile beyond, "yeah, we can be friends again?" Sure, he still loved Ave, but that didn't mean they could ever live together again and it was presumptuous of him to assume Ave still loved him.

He was over-thinking it. Again. Also for the hundredth time.

Ave finally walked through the door and Louis almost fell over with relief. Not that it would be like Ave to pay him back for a no show with a no show, especially in light of his dad's injury, but Louis had still worried in that abstract, "he hates me" way.

"Hey," he said when Ave walked up and smiled at him. Fuck but that smile made his heart pound. He wasn't sure he'd ever see it again, not like that. They went up to order and he knew Ave was talking to him, but he didn't hear a word, just kept staring.

"Are you all right?" Ave finally jolted him out of his stupor by touching his arm, literally making the skin hot.

"Oh! Yeah. I'm sorry, Ave, I was woolgathering."

"You look tired. How's your daddy?"

"Cussing the day I was born and mean as a cottonmouth besides."

Laughing, Ave ordered for both of them, ordering his burger well done with the garden on the side, just like he liked it. "Yeah. He always was a tough old buzzard. Sorry he's laid up, though. That's going to mean a lot of running on your part."

"Nah. Mom rallied the old ladies' aid society to her cause and I only have to go over when she's really upset."

"Oh, cool."

They sat, waiting for their order to be called, and kinda stared at each other. It was awkward, but not as uncomfortable as he might have thought. Just… slow going. Talking still wasn't Louis' strong suit and wishing wasn't going to make it so.

They both drew a breath to speak just about the time their number was called, making them both laugh. They'd sure sat there long enough staring. So they got up and made up their burgers with the ketchup and pickle relish for Ave and the mustard and Duke's relish for Louis and finally broke the ice once they say back down, because Louis' first bite ended up half on his shirt.

"God, Lou, you're such a slob."

Louis winced and looked at Avery, but Ave was laughing, gathering up a handful of napkins and dabbing at Louis' shirt.

"Yeah. Some things never change I guess."

"Would you believe that's kind of comforting?"

That made him loosen his grip on his burger so his tomato slipped out and plopped on his plate. He would never in a million years have thought his slobbiness would be a comfort to Ave. Ever. "Uh."

"Yeah." Ave laughed, only this time it was mostly humorless. "It would still drive me nuts to trip over your wet towels, but perfection? Overrated."

"Having trouble with the new guy?" Unlike the last time they'd talked about it, Louis didn't get snotty and Avery didn't get defensive.

"Kinda. He… well, he doesn't want to meet my Mama, Lou. You know? And he's. Oh, Hell, Gordon is a great guy and he's just what I should want. But he's just not making me happy. Maybe it's me."

Poor Ave looked so worried. Louis shook his head. "Nah. I mean, the kid I hooked up with? Kyle? He's great. Super sweet kid. But Jesus, Ave, I tell you, having another slob around, which I always thought would be so much easier, is tough, because no one fucking cleans and sooner or later I give out before he does and pick up."

They shared a look of complete commiseration and damned if it wasn't fucked up to be bitching with his ex about his and Ave's new things, but it was comfortable, too. Like the lack of their own relationship tension was making it easier for him to talk about shit.

"So, tell me all about the whole estimate thing. Sounds like maybe you won't have to be as physical?"

"I will if you tell me your plans for the new business." He really wanted to hear what Ave was doing with his life. It was definitely a start.

"You got yourself a deal."

Lou grinned, more relieved than he could express. "Cool."

***

Avery just floated back to Justin's apartment. It still wasn't his, wouldn't be no matter how long he crashed there. Home was not a borrowed room with your brother's old baseball trophies on one wall.

Still, he was happier than he'd been in a while. He and Louis had talked. Really talked, about their plans and their dreams and about their current peeves with dating, which was odd, but it had been nice. Damned nice. They'd even gone out for a beer after lunch, just the two of them and a corner of a smoky little bar and while it had been a little awkward, it had been sweet, too.

Maybe they could be friends after all.

And if Avery wanted more than that it was his own fault.

His messages yielded a nosy call from his mother, wanting to know if he'd seen Lou, a call from his brother that was largely unintelligible but meant that Just wouldn't be home, and a call from Gordon that he guiltily ignored. Avery wanted to bask and that was hard to do with Gordon on his mind.

In fact, Avery wanted to bask in the shower, with a bottle of bath oil. Being with Louis, well, friends was what they were going for, yeah, but that didn't stop Avery from remembering how Louis' skin felt, how Louis' cock tasted, and how they fit together. Hell, who was he kidding? Seeing Louis made him want to remember, made him want things, especially since they hadn't argued, had instead talked more than they had in, well, possibly the entire time they'd been together.

The sudden memory of the last time he was in the shower thinking about Louis and touching himself popped up, and it was amazing how one little not-date but meeting could change things. This time he wasn't crying. This time he was on his tiptoes pushing into his hand, breath coming hard, stomach clenching up. This time he wasn't just seeing Louis, he was imagining Louis as a ready participant, on his knees, sucking and touching.

This time, coming felt like coming home, and it scared him to death.

***

"So, have you had sex yet?"

"What?"

Louis' head snapped up and he looked at Kyle, who was grinning at him, licking the stickiness of barbeque ribs off his fingers. They'd ordered in and the remains of cole slaw, hush puppies, and fries were all over the coffee table and the couch.

"Your ex. Avery? Have you two hooked up again yet? You'd be hot together."

He knew he was staring, with his mouth hanging open in what had to be a bad way, but he couldn't help it.

"What makes you think… I mean, why would you?" Louis trailed off, finally, unsure.

"Dude. Mike saw you two together at Fuddrucker's. Are you getting back together?"

"No. I mean. Not. Aren't you upset?" Not that he wanted Kyle to be upset. Louis wasn't the kind to enjoy someone else's jealousy, and he didn't want to hurt the kid. Really.

"Nah." Grinning easily, Kyle set the last rib bone aside and moved to straddle his lap, giving him a greasy, sticky kiss. "I know the score there. He comes back and I'm out. I love you to death, Lou, but you've never been mine."

"Oh." That didn't hurt him, either, but Lou had to admit it baffled him. Which was silly, considering that he knew from the start that Kyle wasn't a permanent type thing for him either. It just seemed… odd to stay with someone when you knew it was just, "So it was just sex?"

"Was? Is. As long as you let me. You're gonna be good for my sexual resume, Lou. You're hot and you know stuff I never even thought of."

Surprised into laughing, Lou grabbed Kyle's shoulders and pulled him down for another kiss, the tang of vinegar and pickles and onions making it spicy. The kid had a point. There was nothing wrong at all with enjoying it, and it took the pressure off, and he'd pretty much been in a state of hyper-aware need since two nights before, so he was going to enjoy it all right, all the way into that tight, hot, little ass.

He and Kyle ended up on the floor with Kyle on his back and Lou between his legs and it was good, not as good as if there was that real connection, he knew, because he knew the difference, but better than it had ever been with Kyle before because it was just for fun, with no worries of the kid getting too attached. Then Kyle started whispering about how maybe it would be really cool to watch him and Ave together, about how pretty they would be, and Louis just lost it, coming like a ton of bricks and not able to do anything at all but watch as Kyle finished himself off.

The whole situation was weird and, if he thought about it too much, it might freak him out more than a little. But all in all, life was getting better every day.

Chapter Seven

"I think it's time I met your mother."

"Pardon?" Avery was blindsided for a moment, not at all sure he'd heard Gordon correctly. They were both reading, the only sound in the room for the last half hour the turning of pages.

"Your mother. You're having brunch with her tomorrow, aren't you?" Those blue eyes peered at him over the top of Gordon's book, and the expression in them made Avery pretty nervous. It was almost sly.

"Yeah. I do that on Sundays."

"So, perhaps I could go with you."

Shifting, Avery set his book aside and folded his arms. "Why?"

"Why?"

"Yes."

Gordon set aside his book as well, and looked at him head on, face set in serious lines. "I think it's time ."

"I'm not trying to upset you, Gordon, but you intimated you didn't want to get that close."

Avery didn't want to get that close either. He knew things with Gordon weren't going well, hadn't been for some time, but especially since he and Louis had started meeting for coffee after class. Three dates they'd had now, if he counted the burger dinner, and each one was better than the last. Unfortunately, the closer he got to Lou again, the more distant he got with Gordon.

"Well, perhaps I have changed my mind." Rising, Gordon came over to him and took his hands, pulling him up into an embrace. "What harm can brunch do?"

"You haven't met my mother."

"Precisely."

While Gordon nuzzled his neck, Avery pondered his choices. He could just say no, but that would be rude, and rudeness just wasn't in his make-up. Not deliberate rudeness anyway. Yet he wasn't sure about taking Gordon to meet his mother at all; it implied a level of relationship they simply didn't have, at Gordon's insistence.

"I'm not sure I…"

"Oh, come, Avery. Don't be rude."

Gordon's voice was one of his best weapons and Avery resented the use of it now, molasses slow and deep against his ear as Gordon nibbled and licked. The feeling that he was being manipulated was strong and he didn't like it. Not one bit.

That didn't mean his body couldn't respond predictably, and it did, his cock rising when Gordon touched it through his pants, rubbing skillfully. Gordon kept at him, touching and

licking and tickling him into a pile of
quivering flesh, then sliding inside him deeply.
As always, Gordon tasted of cigarettes and
whiskey and the kisses were perfect, each one
timed to leave him gasping, each thrust
coordinated to leave him begging for more.

When it was over he felt worse than ever,
but when Gordon kissed his neck and asked
again to meet his mother, Avery simply
nodded and said, "Yeah. Sure."

One day he was going to have to learn to
say no.

***

Louis straightened his tie nervously and
brushed some imaginary lint off his sport coat.
Telling himself he wanted to look nice for
Avery's mama did no good. The primping was
all about Ave and he knew it.

Three dates. Not dates. Whatever. They'd
seen each other socially three times and Louis
got butterflies every time he thought of it. Lord
knew it wasn't that they'd done anything but
talk, but he thought the talking went well. A
lot better than it had the whole time they lived
together. He felt like he was really learning
Ave and not in the touchy feely girly way, just
in the wow you're a cool person way. Maybe
that whole thing about being friends before
you're lovers wasn't all bullshit, because fuck,
he and Ave had skipped the whole friend thing

to begin with in favor of the hot to trot move in with each other thing, and look how that had not worked worth a damn.

Anyway, Ave's mama had called and asked him to join them for brunch, saying she'd missed him, and she knew he and Ave were talking again, so he said yes, and attacked his head with a comb and dressed up like some kind of giant idiot. Fuck, he even put on that cologne Avery liked, the one that Kyle said mixed really well with his musk, whatever that meant, and he had to be the biggest sap ever.

He got to the grill and Avery's mama was there already. She smiled and waved at him and hugged his neck when he got close enough, enthusing over how nice he looked. She smelled like gardenias and looked twice as pretty, and he told her so.

"Oh, now, aren't you the sweetest thing." Esther whapped his arm and he held her chair for her. "Avery is running late, but I saw you coming and ordered you a coffee, cream and sugar, just like you like."

"Thank you, Esther." Sitting perpendicular to Esther, Louis smiled, waiting for the server to leave before plonking his elbows on the table. "So how have you been?"

"Just fine. Avery's daddy had a bit of a sinus infection and I finally took him to the doctor, but he's fine now. It really is distressing how that man holds everything in until he can't hide it anymore, thinking he's protecting me."

There it was, the requisite blush that came with talking to Avery's mama. The gentle rebuke hit home, but Louis just smiled and said, "Well, some folks would rather not worry other folks to death."

"And some folks think it's more worrisome not to know. I'll have the buffet, dear," Esther said, smiling at the waitress, then at him, "I do hope Avery is all right."

So did he. Fervently. As fervently as he hoped Ave would show up soon and distract Esther from her gentle, satiric lecture mode.

As if that thought was a signal, Avery came in just then and Louis' heart leapt, at least until he saw the tall real estate man Ave was dating glide right in behind him. That fucking made a lump settle in his belly. Ave looked as flummoxed as he felt, stopping so abruptly that Guy? Gary? Gordon, that was it, Gordon ran right up his butt.

Even Esther looked taken aback, but she rose to the occasion as beautifully as she always did, standing to kiss Avery's cheek. Louis stood as well, out of habit, and nodded politely. Avery gave him an unreadable look in return and presented his guest.

"Mama, this is Gordon. Gordon, my mother Esther Lakewood. Mama, Gordon Barrister. I think you've met Louis."

"Of course." Gordon smiled at them, taking Esther's hand and bowing over it just slightly, charming as you please. Louis wanted to punch him, or at least tell him he was an unctuous bastard, but he didn't. Go him. "It's a pleasure to meet you, ma'am. Hello again, Louis."

"Hi."

Louis waited for Esther to sit before sinking down into his own chair, trying hard not to let his upset show. There was no use in making waves. He knew very well Ave was still seeing Gordon, just as he was still seeing Kyle. No big deal.

Damn it.

"I hope you don't mind my coming along," Gordon was saying, pausing in an obvious spot so Esther could tell him what to call her.

"Not at all, Gordon. And you can call me Miz Lakewood. I was wondering if Avery was ever going to bring you to meet me."

"Mama…" Avery tried to head Esther off at the pass and Louis figured he wasn't the only one who saw Esther's eyes narrow, or the look that came over her face.

"Now you hush, Avery, and let Gordon and I get acquainted. Why don't you and Louis go fill a couple of plates for us? I'm sure Louis remembers what I like."

Oh, man. More than happy to escape, Louis scraped back his chair and stood while Ave tried one more time.

"Mama…"

"Now, son."

"Yes, ma'am."

They walked away, and Louis winced when he heard Esther's opening salvo of, "So why did you finally decide to invite yourself to meet me, honey?"

Ave was looking kinda green about the gills as they headed for the buffet and Louis actually felt sorry for him. No way could he have known his mama would invite Louis along.

"I'm sorry, Ave. She just up and called this morning. I never thought…"

"Hmm? Oh, of course not, Lou." Avery actually smiled at him, eyes lighting up just like that. "Honestly, I thought he meant it when he said he didn't want to meet her."

"So what changed his mind?"

"I have no idea."

They gathered up food in silence, Louis getting himself eggs and pork fat and biscuits, and getting pancakes and fruit and cottage cheese for Esther. Avery filled two plates as well, one with wheat toast and jam and Eggbeaters, the other with food more like his own. He was filling one of those little cups with butter when Ave moved over close enough to rub hips with him, speaking low-voiced.

"You're not sore at me, are you? I just. Well, I couldn't figure a polite way to tell him no."

Laughing, Louis shook his head, feeling his chest loosen up. "Nah. I kinda feel sorry for him. Your mama is going to tear him to shreds."

To his surprise, Avery laughed too, bumping his butt lightly with one sharp hipbone, almost making him drop his plates.

"Yeah. That was why I decided to bring him."

***

His Mama raked Gordon over the coals about a hundred times in the course of brunch, remaining ever so polite as she told him what she thought of real estate brokers, casual sex, and men who didn't want to meet the families of the folks they dated until the last minute.

Avery would have felt sorry for him, but he would swear Gordon thrived on it, smiling right in the face of every insult and getting so that butter wouldn't melt in his mouth by the end of the meal. It was damned nerve wracking and if it wasn't for the twinkle in Louis' eyes as they snuck looks at each other, he might simply have melted with embarrassment.

They finally finished up their coffee and Avery stood, unable to stay a minute longer. He couldn't talk to Lou, couldn't sit and listen to his Mama and Gordon spar anymore, and if he ate one more apple fritter he was going to explode.

"We need to go, Mama."

"Oh." His Mama stood too, and Gordon and Lou both jumped to their feet. "Well, I'm sorry you can't stay longer, baby. I hope you don't mind if Lou and I stay."

"Why would I?"

Avery stared at her and she smiled benignly and offered her cheek to kiss. Damn her for being up to something. One way or the other, he was going, so let her scheme.

"It was a great pleasure sparring with you, ma'am."

"Oh, maybe you have more brains than I credited you with, Gordon."

Gordon smiled widely. "Oh, I believe I have a lot more going for me than you think."

A snort sounded from Louis' direction, but Avery didn't dare look, as he figured it would make him laugh. So wrapped up was he in keeping his eyes downcast, in fact, that Gordon sliding an arm around his waist and pulling him close came as a complete surprise. Gordon, who was always afraid someone might see.

"You ready to go, love?"

"I. Yes, of course."

They sailed right out of the restaurant like they were on a red carpet somewhere smiling for the cameras, but as soon as they got to the car, Avery pulled away, glaring at Gordon.

"What in Hell has gotten into you?"

A tiny furrow appeared between Gordon's brows, the sound of going to church traffic loud as Gordon paused, obviously considering his words. "I don't know what you mean, Avery."

"Oh, bullshit." Gordon's brows rose, but Ave was beyond caring about his own word choice. "My Mama is the queen of passive-aggressive, Gordon, and you've got nothing on her, so give. What are you doing?"

"I like your Mama very much, by the way. Quite the bastion of Southern womanhood."

"Stop it. Stop it and tell me what's going on."

Gordon was the talker. Gordon wasn't suddenly supposed to be the Louis while Louis turned easy to chat with.

"Must we talk about this here?"

"Yes." He put a hand on Gordon's arm and the muscles there were hard as rocks. "Please."

"Very well, but at least let's get in the car."

They settled into Gordon's SUV, the quiet whoosh of the doors closing shutting out the rest of the world. The only sounds were their breathing and the ticking of the little old-fashioned dash clock Gordon had installed.

"Well?"

"Well. I realized recently that I was going to lose you and the prospect was not a pleasant one for me."

"Lose…" Avery stared, and Gordon had the good grace to flush under his regard. "But you were the one who said."

"I know very well what I said." Gordon snapped it out and it was the first time Avery could remember the man raising his voice. "It's quite the standard speech for me, Avery, and I meant it at the time, but I have grown quite attached to you and have no intention of losing you to your ex."

Avery sat very still, staring, the ticking noise seeming very, very loud. Wasn't that a classic case of you don't know what you have?

"I. I don't know what to say, Gordon. I don't think…"

"Don't."

In a fit of completely uncharacteristic passion, Gordon grabbed him, pulling him halfway across the console, kissing him like there was no tomorrow. The kiss was designed to devastate, and it did, making him breathless and weak, leaving him gasping and clutching Gordon's shoulders. He was so dazed that he almost missed the tiny stiffening of Gordon's muscles, but he managed to look up through the windshield and see Louis staring at them anyway.

Fuck.

Fuck, fuck, fuck.

***

Well. That told him where he stood, didn't it? Louis knew Avery's mama wanted him to stay, but after the whole thing with Avery and the what? Boyfriend? Jealous lover? He just couldn't. So he waited long enough for Avery to be gone, then kissed Esther's cheek and fled, leaving enough cash behind to cover the bill, despite her protests.

He'd though that he and Avery were sharing a joke, no matter how uncomfortable. At the food bar, when they laughed and teased, and later, when Avery kept sneaking looks at him with those bright eyes, they'd seemed in step, on the same page, kinda. So even when he thought he might bust from listening to Esther give Gordon Hell, he just looked at Avery and it was all okay.

Until he walked out of the restaurant and saw them in a fucking lip lock in the car. So much for couldn't find a polite way to say no. That kiss didn't look for a minute like Avery wanted to say no. In fact, when the kiss broke and Avery looked up, he was all flushed and his lips were swollen and Louis knew that look, knew it so well that it made his belly hurt to see someone else put it there. It made him ache and not in a good way.

Louis didn't know why he should be surprised, or worse, hurt. They were just friends, had determinedly said so more than once, and there was no reason at all for his fingers to be shaking as he stumbled to his car, and even less reason to almost get himself killed as he peeled out into traffic. Didn't stop him from doing it though.

The house was so empty it echoed and Louis thought about calling Kyle, but that would be dishonest, maybe as dishonest as he felt Avery was, so he toed off his shoes and settled on the couch to have a nap and watch the game instead. The best thing he could do was not dwell on it, and if he closed his eyes and saw Avery and Gordon kissing on the backs of his eyelids, well, he'd get over it. Just like he had everything else.

Chapter Eight

Gordon was suddenly so attentive and well, domineering, that it was almost a week before Avery got a chance to call Louis, and damned if he didn't get an answering machine. His message went something like, "Hi Lou, I hope we can get together sometime soon," and he left it at that, but he really wanted to say things like, "I'm sorry," and "why haven't you been in class?"

God knew he didn't want to ruin Louis' new shot at education and the new job just by being there. He'd drop the class first, even though they were more than halfway through now.

By the time the next class day rolled around, Avery was almost frantic. He'd called Louis maybe five times and never gotten an answer or a reply. He'd finally grown a pair and told Gordon no, he wasn't coming over after class, in fact he wasn't coming over this weekend at all, and he was waiting for Louis to show up, because if the man didn't appear, Avery was going to go drag him out of his cave by the hair.

Luckily he didn't have to. Louis showed, looking drag ass and worn out, but there, and something loosened in Avery's chest. If he could see Lou they could work it out, but he couldn't do anything if he never got a chance.

Class went by so slowly that Avery thought he might die. The clock on the wall ticked, he could hear it even over the instructor's droning voice and the questions about tax breaks and self-employment taxes, but it was ticking in slow motion. When they were released, Avery sprang up to get out the door first so he could grab Lou on the way out, which was exactly what he had to do, as Lou tried to avoid him.

"Lou, wait. Please."

"Oh. Hey, Ave. I need to…"

"Need to what?" He hated that closed look, remembered it so well, all the more so for not having seen it since they started talking again.

"Go."

"Well, you can't. Not until we talk."

Louis sighed, but with everyone still filing out of the class looking curiously at them, didn't argue. "Yeah, okay. Can we go sit down? I'm beat."

"Sure."

He almost suggested one of their vehicles, but the picture he and Gordon must have presented on Sunday flashed through his mind and he though better of it, leading the way to a deserted hallway and settling on a bench. No one but janitors should be about at this time of the evening, so they should have all the privacy they needed. Only when they sat did he realize he still had a hand on Lou's arm, as if to keep him from bolting.

"Has anything happened with your dad? You look pooped." Avery figured he'd start with something innocuous.

"Nah. He's better. I just had to. Well, a guy at work got sick and the other foreman really needed someone to fill in, so I did some framing and whatever, and I kinda strained my back. But it's feeling better."

Damn. He bit back his instinctive, "are you nuts?" and patted Lou's arm. Louis looked everywhere but at him; the floor, ceiling, and wall over his left shoulder all got close scrutiny. Finally he just put his hand on Louis' cheek and turned Lou's head so they were eye to eye.

"I'm breaking up with Gordon."

"You are? Why? I mean, what happened?"

"Because perfect gets on my nerves."

"As much as slobby?"

Lou looked chastened right after he said it, but Avery really didn't blame him for saying it. "The messiness wasn't so much it and you know it."

"It didn't look like you were breaking up at brunch the other day."

"I know." Grimacing, Avery shrugged. "He got all possessive on me, Lou. Told me he wasn't going to lose me to you and that's when it occurred to me that I was never his to lose. You know?"

"No. I don't." If anything Lou looked more tired and confused.

"I never invested in the relationship, Lou. I was still hung up on you."

Something sharp and hot flared in Louis' eyes, making the green stand out from the gray and gold. "Don't go there, Ave. I can't take the roller coaster."

"I'm not. I'm just telling you."

There was a tension in the air that hadn't been there a minute before, though, so whether he meant it as a declaration or not, it became one. The hard bench under his butt and the buzzing of the one fluorescent light that was trying to burn out went away and he focused on Louis. He focused on Louis' soft mouth and sharp collarbones and how Louis smelled just like the same cologne and sawdust man he'd always been.

Lou's voice got very low, deep and husky. "Please, Ave. I... I can't."

"Okay. It's okay."

Avery moved back an inch, maybe two, letting his hand fall to Louis' shoulder, where the muscles were rock hard with tension. Poor Lou, working so hard and trying so hard and then him coming along and tying Lou all up knots again.

"I'm sorry," he said, and he wasn't sure if he meant for Gordon, or for leaving, or for wanting.

"I know. Me too, Ave."

The skin under his fingers felt almost fevered and a muscle jumped at the base of Louis' neck. "Do you think... I mean can we. Damn it, Lou, can we go out on a date? A real one, not just a coffee thing? Maybe this weekend?"

"A date." Eyes searching his, Louis turned to face him fully, leaning in. "You and me? I haven't even broken up with Kyle.'

"Oh." Well, that rocked him back on his figurative heels. He hadn't even thought Louis might be unwilling to let the kid go. Lou had bitched about Kyle being even messier than Louis, but that didn't mean there wasn't something there. "Are you going to? I mean, I'm sorry, that's none of my business."

The old fashioned Southern formality was back in his voice; he couldn't help it, when you fucked up, you fell back on manners. Louis just grimaced.

"Don't you get snooty with me."

"I'm not. I just. I was hoping so hard."

"Well, I like the kid, okay? So I don't know. I mean, fuck, Ave, neither he nor I are serious about it, but he's a good, uncomplicated fuck. And you're complicated."

"I know." He sat back even further, arms crossed over his chest now, a knot of misery in his belly. "I'm still breaking up with Gordon."

"Good. He's a prick."

Surprised, he barked out a laugh. "Yeah. Even more than I am."

"Oh, Ave. You're not a prick." Lou put a hand over one of his, pulling at it, and he had to unclench it so Lou could hold it. "At least not like that. I just can't go so fast. I still hurt from last time."

"So you'll think about it?" If he could at least get Lou to think about it, to agree to try, he was better off than he ever hoped to be.

"Yeah. I'll think about it."

"Good."

They were quiet after that and they sat there in the silence for a long time before they got up to go their separate ways. Louis held his hand all of the way out to the parking lot, too, and it gave him hope. Now all he had to do was make good on breaking up with Gordon, which might prove easier said than done.

***

"What's eating you?"

"With any luck, you will be." Man, that came out fucking lame. Louis tried to pass off Kyle's question, but he just couldn't. Even three days later he was still reeling from his talk with Avery. He just couldn't wrap his mind around the wild hope that had sprung up, and how he'd quashed it firmly because he just couldn't take it if Avery came back only to leave again the first time he screwed up.

"Very funny," Kyle said, bringing him back to the present. "Seriously, you're all bear grouchy."

"Avery asked me out on a date." There. It was out and he felt oddly bad, even though Kyle knew all about him and Ave, and knew things might be happening there again.

"Cool. You going to go?"

"I don't know."

"What?" They'd just finished dinner, and Kyle shoved the Hardee's bags off on the floor, moving close to him and putting a hand on his leg, just below the opening of his boxers. "You gotta, Lou. You're still so hung up on him it hurts, man."

"That doesn't mean I need to go running back to him."

Damn. How surreal could it get? The kid was pushing him to go back to his ex. Weird.

"No. I know, but you two just needed to get to know each other again, right? And you've been doing that."

"You're not helping my ego, kid."

"Oh, Louis." Kyle grinned at him, fingers walking up his leg to slide under the cotton covering his thigh. "You know I dig you. But I actually like you, too, okay? And I think you really love this guy and you miss him and you need to decide if he's worth working for."

Louis let his legs fall open, let Kyle touch him, moaning at the feel of those hot fingers closing around him. Kyle was right, he did need to make a decision, and weird as it was to be thinking about taking up with his ex again while another guy held his dick, that was just what he did. Was Ave worth trying to salvage? Even a month ago he might have said no, but that was when he was still angry. Now? He knew he wanted to try.

"Okay. I'll go on a date with him."

"Cool. And maybe when you guys get back together? You could invite me over to play."

Lord, the kid was fixated on that, wasn't he, but even Louis had to admit it was a pleasant thought, seeing Kyle going down on Avery, or maybe Avery fucking Kyle's round ass. Damn. Louis shuddered, his cock pounding with his heartbeat, swelling to fill Kyle's hand.

"Yeah," he said, gasping. "Maybe."

"Even if I just watched that would be cool. He's pretty, you know? Bet he takes it from you even better than I do."

God, he was going to explode. Just blow all over. Louis reached for Kyle, pulling that athletic young body close, tugging at Kyle's t-shirt. The feel of Kyle's skin, warm and damp, mixed with the thought of Avery's ass in the air, taking it from him as he pushed in hard, and Louis humped against Kyle, letting all of the stress and ache go, letting his mind stop working and his body take over.

Kyle talked, saying filthy things, shit he didn't even know the kid knew, and before long it was over, and they were a sticky mess of arms and legs and hot breath.

"You'll call him?"

"Yeah. Yeah, I'll call."

"Cool."

***

The scene was set. Dinner. Wine. Guilt.

Avery waited for Gordon to come home, knowing he was using his spare key and his eagerness to get this over with as an unfair advantage to ambush the man when he walked in the door, but he couldn't help it. He'd promised to break up with Gordon. Heck, he wanted to, but it still didn't make him feel any better about it.

When the door opened he got that socked in the stomach feeling and Avery braced himself to get through this, just holding his head up and smiling, looking Gordon right in the eye. Gordon smiled back, coming over to offer him a kiss, which he took on the cheek instead of the lips.

"You made me dinner."

"Yes. Would you like a glass of wine?" He ignored Gordon's frown, listening to his heartbeat in his ears. This was nothing like breaking up with Lou. That was unpremeditated and heart-rending. This was just nerve-wracking and sad.

"That would be nice, yes." Tie and briefcase went into the seat of a living room chair and Gordon went into the other while Avery got the wine. They sat for a while, not really talking but for the usual "how was your day" sort of stuff, and finally the timer went off in the kitchen, making Avery sigh in relief. His nerves were clearly showing, but Gordon was too polite to mention it, simply exclaiming over the quality of the wine.

"I'm glad you like it. I used it on the beef as well."

"Excellent."

They sat and ate, the conversation stilted but the food good, and when it was over Avery figured he had enough wine in him to find his courage.

"Gordon, there's something I'd better speak to you about."

"I see. So serious. I take it this is where you give me the we should be friends speech."

His cheeks heated. "Well, I would hope we could remain friends, but yes, I don't think we should see each other romantically anymore."

"I thought that was what this was about. How droll. A bit obvious, don't you think?" Gordon's tone left a lot to be desired; it was downright ugly, but Avery told himself the man was hurt, in pride if nothing else, and tried to let it go.

"Well, never say I'm not old-fashioned. Look, Gordon, I think it's pretty clear that we're not going anywhere…"

"And you wish to be free to pursue your ex."

"Well, yes, not to put too fine a point on it." If Gordon could be blunt as a rock upside the head, so could he.

"He's only going to cause you pain, you know. You should have learned by now that he's just not the right type for you."

"That's really not the point. I just don't think you're the one for me either, Gordon."

Saying that, and so bluntly too, made him feel horrible, rude and cruel, but Avery was on the defensive and didn't quite know how to deal with Gordon's whole attitude. If the man had yelled, like Lou, or clammed up, like his dad, or even gotten sweet as pie, like his mom did when she was mad, he might know what to do. Instead, Gordon got businesslike, hard-faced and impassive.

"I see. Well, as you say." Gordon stood abruptly, his crumpled linen napkin falling to the floor, and it seemed odd to Avery when Gordon did not immediately pick it up. "I think you should go now."

"Of course." Just as wooden, Avery climbed to his feet. "Let me just get my things."

"Now, Avery. I want you to leave now."

"But I just need to get my clothes and my…"

"Now."

Catching him completely unawares, Gordon took his arm and propelled him through the perfectly decorated living room, handing him his coat and opening the door to shove him through. Avery dug in his heels, wanting to at least get his shaving kit, which sat in Gordon's bathroom defiantly, one of the few things the man had let him move in.

"Gordon, please, at least let me..."

The door clicked shut in his face. Avery looked about to make sure no one was watching, his compulsively Southern upbringing making him nervous about making a scene. Still, his shaving kit was in there and more importantly his cell phone and his keys. He knocked softly.

"Gordon, come on. My keys and stuff are in there."

There was no answer for a long time, but finally the door opened and a plastic bag flew out at him. Luckily his reflexes kicked in and he caught it, finding not only his phone and his keys, but his toothbrush and his shaving kit and a few other small things. Gordon didn't even look at him, just shut the door back and the sound of the deadbolt clicking locked was very loud in the silence that ensued.

Chapter Nine

"Hello?" Lou blinked at the clock as he fumbled with the phone to get the handset where he could hear the person on the other end. Damn. He'd fallen asleep on the couch and it was about ten at night now. He'd never get to sleep when he went to bed.

"Hey, Lou."

Avery's voice was all he needed to wake up, heart speeding.

"Hey. You okay?"

"Yeah. I guess. Can I come over?"

"What? Why? What's wrong, Ave?" Damn, he was loggy-headed, and now he was worried. Avery sounded really strained.

"I broke up with Gordon."

"Oh." Well. What was he supposed to say to that? He wanted to sort of jump up and down and say 'fucking A', but at the same time, he wasn't sure how he felt about Ave being completely free again. "No."

"What?"

"No, you can't come over."

"But, Lou."

"No. I'm sorry, Ave, but I can't be the rebound for your rebound break-up, if that makes sense."

"It doesn't."

It probably didn't make sense, but he wanted Avery to come over because he wanted to, because he wanted to see him, Louis, not because he was reeling from a breakup with someone else.

"Well, I'm sorry, Ave. I just can't. Now, if you were to ask me out on a date again, a real date, not just coffee, I might say yes."

"Yeah?" Oh, there was a world of breathless wonder there and it almost broke his resolve not to let Ave come over right then and there, but Louis wanted to take it slow. No more rushing in and no more false hope.

"Yeah. I just can't see you tonight, though, Ave. Do you get why?"

"I do." Avery sighed, and Lou bit back a chuckle at the long-suffering sound. "I don't like it, but I get it."

"Good. So how about next weekend? Saturday?"

"Okay. I'll take you out to dinner."

Louis had a thought and whether it was a good one or not, it stuck with him. "No. I'll cook."

"You will?"

"Sure. Can you be here at say, seven?"

"You bet."

"Okay. See you in class."

"You sure will."

Louis laughed, feeling like he'd lightened Avery's load and definitely feeling lighter himself. "Night, Ave."

"Night, Lou. And thanks."

"No problem, babe."

They hung up and Louis sat staring at the wall for a while before he realized he was grinning like an idiot. And that he'd agreed to cook. He'd have to go shopping for Brunswick stew ingredients before the next weekend. Lord knew, courting Avery this time around ought to be easier, because this time? He knew what Avery liked.

***

Lou was going to cook for him. That wasn't just a good sign. It was a great one. It made the embarrassment of his scene with Gordon and his sadness at the way it ended too, he wasn't that big of a prick, ease. A lot. He did understand why he couldn't just go over there and, while it stung for the first few minutes after Louis said no, Avery got it. He did.

Justin's apartment was even more depressing than usual tonight, frighteningly dull as he let himself in, quiet but for Just's snoring, and smelling like dirty socks. Gross. Avery went right to his room, stripping off before heading for a shower. He felt like washing Gordon off, which was silly, and probably mean as Hell, because the man had every right to be hurt, but damn, that had been nasty. Nasty in an aggressive, worried for his safety sort of way. He never would have thought the perfect, urbane Gordon would have it in him, and Avery certainly never thought of himself as the kind to inspire such possessiveness.

It was plain weird.

He scrubbed good, resolutely thinking of other things. His upcoming date with Louis was foremost on his mind, but Avery pushed that aside too, knowing he couldn't get too excited about it, or it would end up being a disaster of nerves and crossed signals. Louis had drawn a definite line in the sand as far as how fast they were going was concerned and he was determined to honor it. So Avery thought about his new business venture instead, and his dad's invitation to join the bowling league, and his brother's… Shit!

Cold water. Really freaking cold water that made him gasp and splutter and Avery yanked back the curtain to find Justin laughing at him like a loon while the toilet flushed.

"Just wanted to make sure you weren't choking the chicken in my shower."

"You are foul."

"Is that f-o-w-l, or…" Justin ran, dodging the bottle of shampoo easily, and Avery rinsed off, stepping out of the shower and drying off, figuring he might as well just give up and go to

bed. At least thanks to his skanky brother he
went laughing and not depressed as anything.

***

They saw each other in class. They called
each other on the nights they weren't in class.
Every time Avery tried to steer the
conversation toward the really personal, Louis
steered it away, and he knew that frustrated
Ave, it always had. He didn't want Ave to
think he was falling back into old habits, the
ones where he didn't talk, but Louis was
determined to take it slow this time, if there
was a this time, and not blow it.

Louis cleaned. He cleaned until the kitchen
sparkled and the floor shone, and he even had
Kyle help him hang new curtains. He stuffed
the kid's oversized sneakers in the guest room
closet when he realized they were still there
and put his grandma's tablecloth on the table.

He cooked, too. Louis thought seriously
about making chicken and dumplings, or
lasagna, or something not stew, because Lord
knew there was baggage attached there, but he
finally decided to go on ahead because he
knew how much Avery liked it, and it was
something he was good at, after all.

The first time he'd made it for Avery had
almost been a disaster because he was so
nervous and so busy thinking about how it
might not measure up to Avery's mama's that

he'd forgotten the tomatoes and the lima
beans. Luckily, Avery had called and told him
he would be late and Louis had gone to see if
the pot needed more salt and discovered his
mistake. The tomatoes were still a little firm,
but Avery didn't seem to notice, and the smile
he got for his effort had made it all
worthwhile.

This time was no better. Louis didn't forget
any ingredients, but he was just as nervous,
just as twitchy, and when he caught himself
fluffing the pillows like Suzy Homemaker he
figured it was time for a distraction. He called
his mother.

"Hello?"

"Hey, mom."

"Louis, honey! How are you? Oh, it's good
of you to call."

Blinking, Louis tucked the phone under his
ear and started chopping little pieces of parsley
for the stuffed mushroom caps he was making
as an appetizer. "How's everything with dad?
Is he healing up all right?"

"Well, you know your daddy. He's tough.
They thought maybe he was going to have an
infection, but he fought it off. Mrs. Demers
came by yesterday and brought him a
chocolate cream pie. Wasn't that nice of her?
He just grunted at her, but I thought it was the
sweetest thing."

His mom chattered on and on, telling him
all about the church ladies, and his dad, and

about the chipmunk that got stuck in the down spout of the gutter, and he uh huh-ed in all the right places.

"Louis, honey, are you still there?"

"Sure mom, I was just listening. I don't think I've ever heard you go on so."

"Well, honey, you never call. And I always feel like I'm imposing when I do, so I wait until I have something important."

Now that was even more of a blinker. Was that why it seemed like his mom never called unless she needed something? Because she was afraid to disturb him?

"Am I that much of a bastard, mom?"

"Louis! You watch your mouth."

"Yes, ma'am. Sorry."

"Well, it's all right. And no, honey, you're not." She paused and he would swear he could hear her thinking hard, like grinding gears. His mom wasn't given to thinking before she spoke, but in this case, he appreciated it. "I just know it's hard, what with the way your daddy and you don't get along, and I know you don't like church and the things I like to do. It's easier not to, is all."

He was saved from both introspection and answering by a knock on the door. "There's my dinner date, mom. Talk to you later, okay?"

"Okay, honey. Have a good time. I love you."

"Love you, too."

They hung up just as Avery knocked again
and Louis had to smile at the way that knock
ended more abruptly than it should. Ave hated
to be rude and Lou would bet his impatience
was at war with his good manners. He took a
deep breath and opened the door and oh. That
was a sight for sore eyes.

Avery looked good. So good. His thick
blond hair was combed straight back off his
forehead, emphasizing the clean lines of his
cheeks and chin, and his eyes, those whiskey
eyes, all full of hope and fear and something
Louis was afraid to think of just made him
want to grab Avery and kiss him and forget all
about boundaries and going slow.

Too bad he knew he couldn't.

"Hey. You, um, going to let me in?"

"Huh? Oh! Yeah." Duh. Louis backed off,
letting the door swing wide. Avery came in,
eyeing the room curiously and Louis took the
time to admire the way Avery's chinos clung
to his ass.

"You got new curtains."

"Yeah, well, you know how old and dingy
the other ones were. You want a drink?"

That was it. He needed to find something to
do with his hands. Without thinking he made
himself a scotch on the rocks and Avery a gin
and tonic with some lime, which was a far cry
from the beer he and Kyle had been drinking
since they met up. Louis had gone by the
liquor store and stocked up.

"Oh, thanks." He got a beaming smile. "You remembered."

"Well, it hasn't been that long Ave."

He could have bitten his tongue when Avery's face fell and Avery shrugged. "It's been long enough."

"Yeah." Fuck. Brilliant. That was what he was. "So, uh. Tell me about your new business?"

The smile came back and Avery nodded, plopping down on the couch and crossing his legs. "It's really cool. I'm doing these great curb appeal projects, you know? And my favorites are in the old neighborhoods, where I get to work with what's there and clean it up and make it showy again. We have some of the prettiest flowering trees and shrubs in this area, you know? I had forgotten how pretty an azalea could be. Working with indoor plants just isn't the same."

Wow. Avery's eyes just shone with pure pleasure; it was a beautiful thing to see. "So have you quit the day job?"

"No. I'm still working for them half time until my own business is up and supporting me. Which is close. My boss, he's been great."

"You always did like him."

"Yeah." Avery grinned at him. "So what about you? How's the appraisal business?"

"Good, now that the crew is straightened out and I'm not working part time on the framing anymore."

The lines around Avery's mouth tightened, but Ave didn't say a word, just sipped his drink and nodded. That was a relief, because he hated defending himself, but Louis found himself talking about it anyway. "I talked to the big boss, told him I was happy to help out, but I just couldn't do that kind of work anymore, and since he was the one who promoted me, he should trust me to hire someone new when we were short-handed."

"Yeah? That's great, Lou. I'm proud."

Heaving a sigh of relief, Louis nodded, smiling. "So, you want to try my mushrooms?"

***

The stuffed mushroom caps tasted earthy and meaty and just delicious, and Avery told Louis so.

"Thanks." Louis grinned at him, green eyes bright. "I've been practicing."

"Well, practice makes perfect." He hid a wince, knowing that was probably a dumb thing to say, but Louis didn't bat an eye, so Avery let it go happily.

The place looked good. Really good. Clean and bright, not a wet towel on the floor anywhere. Smelled good, too, like Brunswick stew and biscuits and something sweet. Something vaguely berry-ish that he was hoping was a strawberry roll.

"Is that strawberry roll I smell?"

"Yeah." A blush rose on Louis' cheeks. "I know how you like it."

Did he ever. The very first time he'd had it, Louis had brought it back from his mom's church to-do. Strawberry roll was mainly pie crust, rolled out thin and spread with butter, sugar, and strawberries in juice, then rolled like a jelly roll and baked. Sweet enough to send you bouncing off the walls, but oh, so good. Every time Lou had gone to take his mom to church after that Avery had asked for it, finally prompting Louis to learn to make it.

"I do like it. Thank you. Would you come sit with me?" Louis was fluttering. That's what his mama would call it, just flitting around all nervous, and Avery wanted him to be comfortable. Sure, it was awkward and strange, him finally being back in the house, but they had to start somewhere.

"Oh. Sure." Louis sat next to him on the couch, just far enough away that their legs didn't touch, and Avery just wanted to crawl into his lap and kiss him, but he didn't, popping another mushroom instead.

"So, how's your mother? And your daddy? Is he getting on all right?"

"Dad had an infection. But Mom says he's okay now. I called her today, just before you came. She seemed really surprised."

The faintly perplexed look on Lou's face made him want to laugh, but he didn't, figuring that would hurt Lou's feelings.

Instead he patted Lou's knee and said, "Well, you aren't the most forthcoming person, Lou. She was probably tickled."

"She was." Lou stared at his hand and that knee started jiggling under his fingers, bouncing up and down nervously.

"Am I bothering you?"

"No. I just... dinner ought to be ready."

Lou jumped up, and Avery stood as well, blocking his path so that Lou ran right into him. Taking shameless advantage, Avery put his hands on Louis' narrow hips to steady him and leaned in, stealing a kiss that made both of them gasp.

"Ave. Please."

"Please what?"

"Please don't. Not yet. I. We need to have dinner, and talk and shit."

"You still taste just as good."

"Stop it." Pushing away, Louis backed up a few steps, arms crossing over his chest. "Please. Just stop."

He knew he was pushing too far, too fast, but he couldn't seem to help it. Drawing a deep breath, Avery spoke sternly to his other brain and nodded. "I'm sorry, Lou."

"I'm not. But we can't do that yet."

Well, that was a start. Not as good a one as he would have liked. But a start. " Well, let's do dinner then."

"Cool."

***

The stew came out great and the biscuits were fluffy. The strawberry roll was a triumph and when they were done, Louis could swear he saw a bulge in Avery's tummy, just like a bird's gullet after eating a fish. Not that Avery was remotely birdlike, not the way he ate. More like a fox and that image worked for the way he'd snuck in that kiss, too.

That kiss that did more for him in five seconds than Kyle had done for him in six months.

Which made him think of Avery's other man. "So it was bad, huh? You and Gordon?"

Blinking rapidly, Avery sipped his coffee before answering. "Yeah. I mean not exactly homicidal mania or anything, but he kicked me out of his place right away, hollered at me pretty good. Threw all of my stuff out in the hall."

"Made a scene."

"Yes."

There was a wealth of meaning in that single word and Louis' reactions were just as complex. He wanted to be mean and say how sad it was that Avery's perfect man threw him out. He wanted to sympathize and say he knew how Avery hated a scene. And he wanted to go over to Gordon's place and beat the man to a bloody pulp.

He settled for, "Bummer."

"Yeah. Not that I didn't want to break off with him. I was just hoping it could be civilized."

"Right."

"So what about you and, um. Kyle?"

The words were casual, but the body language told an entirely different story, Avery not meeting his eyes, muscles tight, legs crossing.

"I told you I was still seeing him."

"You did."

The words just dropped like lead balloons. Louis sighed. " I'm not trying to bust your balls, Ave. The sex is good and it comes without strings."

"That's what I thought with Gordon."

"Kyle's different."

"How can you be sure?"

"Because he wants to watch us have sex."

Avery stared at him, eyes wide, for what had to be a full minute, spluttering. Then Ave just cracked up, bending over and holding his ribs, howling with laughter. "Oh, God. That's priceless."

"Yeah. I thought so, too." Louis found himself smiling along, pushing away the lingering heat of that image with reluctance. "So are you convinced?"

At length Avery sobered, dried his eyes. "I might be if you kissed me."

Oh, God. "Ave."

"Just a kiss. Please?"

He wanted to, so bad. But he wasn't sure he could without ruining it, without just breaking all of his promises to himself. Avery looked so hurt, so please and thank you, though, that he had to try. "Just one."

They met in the middle of the sofa, Avery's hand coming up to cup his cheek, fingers sliding into his hair as their lips came together, soft and smooth, blending like they'd never been apart. It was enough to bring fucking tears to his eyes. He still loved Ave, no doubt about it. So much.

This time he tried to deepen the kiss and Ave was the one to pull back, fingers sliding along his lips, pushing in to feel his teeth.

"I should go, shouldn't I?"

"If we want this date to end successfully, yeah." Hardest fucking thing in the world to say, but true. If they were going to follow his getting to know you plan, yeah. True.

"I love you, Lou. Don't ever doubt that for a moment."

That fucking shattered him, left him blinking back those damned tears that he didn't even know he had left in him. "I love you, too, Ave. But we…"

"Shh." Avery's fingers pressed his lips together, shushing him. "I know. Now kiss me goodnight and show me the door."

The last kiss was sweet, a little sad, a lot salty. They walked to the door together,

Avery's hand on his arm, petting. Soothing. "Night, Ave."

"Goodnight, Louis. Dinner was amazing. I'll see you in class?"

"Yeah. You sure will."

"Good."

The door opened and closed on a burst of cool, early spring night air and Avery was gone.

Well. That had gone well, hadn't it?

Chapter Ten

Digging in the dirt gave Avery a sense of intense satisfaction. The weeds and kudzu that choked the azalea plant gave way beneath his spade, leaving him feeling accomplished, proud. It also got out aggressions. Of any kind. In this case they were twofold. Avery wanted to throttle Justin and he wanted to fuck Louis. The latter could be more or less solved with some lotion and his hand. The former? Well, that was why he was out digging in his mama and daddy's yard.

"Avery, honey? Do you want some lemonade? Or some iced tea?"

Chuckling, Avery stuck his spade in the soil and stood, dusting off hands and knees. He should have known his mama wouldn't wait too long to poke at him. "Some lemonade, mama. Just let me wash off."

"No hurry, honey."

Which meant 'get your ass up here on the porch and talk to me'.

He hurried, washing off in the stream of lukewarm water from the garden hose before joining his mama on the porch. She had lemonade and sun tea and those little sandwiches of hers, and Avery figured he was about to get the third degree.

"Well, this is nice, mama, but I don't see..."

"Hush. It's not like you to be dense, Avery, and I won't believe it now. So, tell me what's going on."

"Well," he took a sip of lemonade, thinking fast. "Just and I are going to tie it up, mama. He's making me crazy."

She gave him a look, but didn't call him on his evasion, simply picked up a sandwich and nibbled before pointing out, "Well, he probably wants to be alone with his new girl. I imagine it's hard on him, too, baby."

Oh. Well, that was probably true. Avery rubbed his temples, feeling suddenly tired. "Am I that selfish?"

His mama just laughed, the sound low and not a bit mocking. "Oh, honey, we all are. You have your new business and your classes and your man problems to worry on. And Justin has his job, which you know he's not fond of, and his new lady friend he wants to impress. So you're going to get on each other's nerves, aren't you?"

"Yeah. Yeah, I guess so."

"So, did you break up with that awful Gordon?"

She poured out more lemonade while he stared at her. Smiling, she handed him the glass, pushing a plate of cucumber sandwiches over as well, waiting patiently. Lord, you had to love her.

"Yes, mama. I. Well, I had a date with Lou last week."

"Oh? How did that go?"

There was no way she was pulling off that innocent, uninterested tone. Avery grinned at her, shaking his head. "Now, mama."

"Just tell me, Avery."

"He made me Brunswick stew."

She clapped her hands, laughing. "Oh, good."

"That doesn't mean anything."

"Of course not, dear. Have another sandwich."

Well. She looked so happy for him that he didn't have the heart to try and caution her not to get her hopes up, so Avery just had another sandwich, trying to decide whether he wanted snap dragons around her front border, or petunias. He thought maybe purple petunias.

***

The pounding of nails into wood and the hum of circular saws were so familiar that Louis hardly noticed them anymore. The only thing weird about it these days was that he wasn't the one making all the noise. He was impressed with the new guys he'd hired to do framing and the finishing guy was fantastic. Not only that, but Greenville was booming as far as building went, and Louis had a feeling they would get a nice bonus this quarter.

"Hey, Lou. Come on up to the trailer and talk to me a minute."

"Sure."

Hoping he wasn't about to get his bubble burst, Lou followed his boss, Frank, back to the little office trailer set up on site, closing the door behind him and shutting out most of the noise.

"Something wrong?"

"Hell, no. I just wanted to tell you what a damned good job I think you're doing. You were right. There was no way I should have asked you to go back on crew. Hiring Andy and Rick was a fine decision."

Pleased and proud, Louis nodded. "Yeah, they're good guys."

"They are. So are you about done with those classes?"

Searching Frank's round, pleasant face got him nowhere, so Louis just nodded. "Yeah. 'Bout another two weeks, then finals."

"Excellent."

That big old cat and canary grin made him nervous as anything. "Frank, you're scaring the crap out of me. What 's going on?"

"Louis, my boy, I think come the end of the fiscal year you've earned a vacation. I want you to plan on at least two weeks with pay."

He blinked. Blinked some more, not quite
sure he was hearing right. "Are you sure? I
mean, there's bound to be work then, and..."

"You saying you don't want time off, boy?"

"No, sir." The response was as immediate
as it was humiliating. Frank sounded like his
dad. It was kind of baffling.

"Good. Then just tell me when you'd like to
have off after the first of July."

"Um. Probably sometime in September?
Can I look at the calendar and let you know?"

"You bet." One big hand fell on his good
shoulder, clapping it roughly. "Good work,
Louis. Damned good work."

Blush heating his cheeks, Louis ducked his
head, grinning. "Thanks, boss."

"No problem."

***

Avery was on his way out to class when he
passed Justin's bedroom and noticed his little
brother primping in the mirror, combing his
hair this way and that, checking it to make sure
it laid flat. That gave him pause and he
knocked hesitantly, remembering what his
mama had said about selfish.

"Hot date?"

"Yeah. With Emily."

Heck, he had no idea who Emily even was,
but Avery smiled and nodded. "Look, uh. I've
got class tonight, and then if you wanted I

could stay at Mama and Daddy's tonight. You know. If you wanted me to."

That garnered him a wide-eyed stare, a bright, dawning smile. "Yeah? Oh man, that would be awesome. Emily has a roommate and man am I sick of making out in the car."

Just had the good grace to blush after that one, but Avery just laughed. "No problem. I won't be back until tomorrow afternoon then."

"I owe you one."

"Good. Pick up your socks."

He left Just chuckling and detoured back past his room to pick up a change of clothes, happy that he did something a little less about him for a change.

***

When Louis got to class, Avery was already there, sitting at the back. The smile he got when Avery looked up and noticed him made his belly tight, and his own answering smile stretched his cheeks so he thought they would break.

"This seat taken?" he asked, pointing to the chair next to Ave's, and Ave shook his head.

"Nope. I was kinda hoping you'd take it."

"Cool."

They had to pay attention after that, because no way was Louis going to mess up his A average, not after surprising himself with it and working so hard, but he was still acutely aware of Avery sitting right next to him, their feet almost touching. It was somehow more intimate than if they'd been in each other's laps. Louis resisted the urge to play footsie by taking detailed notes, writing down everything he would need to know for his final, which was going to be a bookkeeping mock-up rather than a test. Hands on, just like he liked it.

Even with all of the concentration and with ignoring Avery studiously, Louis was half hard by the time class was over, just knowing that he and Ave were working toward, what? Something, anyway, was making him horny. Really horny. Damn it.

"Huh?" He just realized he'd missed whatever Ave said to him as the class let out, the other folks shuffling papers and putting away books.

"I said do you want to go get coffee and pie or something?"

Poor Ave looked a little red in the face and Lou figured it wasn't really because of him, more's the pity. He knew that hangdog look.

"Can't go home, huh?"

"I promised Just the place to himself tonight. But you know I would have asked you anyway."

"I know, Ave, you just do guilt like no one else I know."

God, it was good to smile together, to laugh and let it be easy and simple. His dick subsided a little and he was damned grateful that he could stand. They started out together, heading for the commuter lot, and Avery's hand brushed the small of his back, making the hair on his arms stand up.

"I know. So, pie?"

"Sure. Look, why don't you just come on back to my place? I have some cookies and milk." He wasn't sure why he'd asked, as it went beyond their established boundaries in a big way, but he did, and he wouldn't take it back. Avery stopped, pulling him to a halt, too, and turned him so they stood face to face.

"I'm not sure I can without... well, wanting things, Lou."

Well, that was honest. Those brown eyes were just staring right at him, trying to crack him open and see inside, he thought. Hell, Louis wanted things, too, lots of them, and maybe it was time he got them. Maybe he was just holding back too much for nothing. All of the maybes swam in his head, making more noise than a full crew on a new house deadline.

He shook it off, finding concern in Avery's eyes when he looked up again. "Lou?"

"I think I want things too, Ave. I'm just not sure it's the right time."

Avery nodded, reaching out to touch his arm, fingers lingering. 'Then we go have pie. At the Huddle House or something. And I go to Mama and Daddy's and you go home. I'm not going to push."

"But see, that's why I want... Hell, Ave, when you were pushing too fast I was worried. Now you're all gentlemanly and I want to jump you. Fuck if I don't sound like a girl."

"You don't."

They grinned at each other, shifting foot to foot, both of them blushing and Louis feeling awkward as all Hell. Finally, Louis just jerked his head toward his car. "Come and sit with me and we'll talk about pie."

"Okay."

They got into the car, both of them sitting and staring straight ahead, Louis with his hands on the wheel, Avery's folded primly. Avery was grinning, though; he could see it out of the corner of his eye.

"So you want to jump me, huh?"

"Hell, yes."

He turned and so did Ave, like they were doing some choreographed dance, and his left hand found Avery's cheek, Ave's coming up to the back of his neck, and they were kissing. Sweet, achingly familiar, slow as molasses in winter, the kiss opened him up like Avery's stare hadn't been able to a while back, cracking his reserve and making him crazy for it.

Louis shifted, pushing Ave back toward the passenger window, deliberately not thinking about the time he'd seem Avery and Gordon kissing in Gordon's perfect SUV. Ave was here, with him. Had broken up with Gordon mainly for him. It meant something. Meant a lot.

Avery's arms slid around his back, clutching him and he crawled over the console, the two of them barely fitting in the seat, his feet dangling and awkward, tilting him forward at an odd angle. It didn't matter, though, because it put him in the lee of Avery's spread thighs, and Lord knew how Ave had managed to squirm around like that, but he had. They were chest to chest and hip to hip, his rough stubble turning Ave's cheeks bright red, his hands coming up to twine in Ave's messy, blonde waves.

They were probably being stupid. Probably needed to slow down, but oh, it felt so good. So well remembered that it might have been yesterday that they'd done this, not almost a year. They moved together in a frenzy, the stiff bulge of Avery's cock hard against his lower belly, his own cock hard enough to make his jeans damned uncomfortable, and all of his encounters with Kyle seemed suddenly pale, like he'd finally figured out what was missing. Or at least admitted to himself he'd known what was missing all along.

Avery's head smacked against the window, pinning Louis' hand behind it, making them both grunt. Avery's hands slid down his back to his ass, palms fitting around each cheek, fingers massaging the undersides through his jeans, and Louis knew right then this would be short and violent. He struggled, rearing back, getting his jeans open, attacking Avery's. Ave moaned, licked those kiss-swollen lips, and Louis groaned, falling back down on Avery and humping like a mad thing, both of them gasping, his reflection in the window showing him wide-eyed and open-mouthed.

"Oh. Oh, God, Lou. I can't. Gonna. Oh."

Fuck. That was Avery's need to come face and Louis kissed that mouth, kissed hard enough to see stars, his cock so tight it hurt. The heat and wetness of Avery's come hit him, burning his skin, making him want to wail, but he hid the shout in the kiss, hips jerking wildly as he came with a violence that left him stunned and panting.

Wow. Oh, wow. That? Was definitely too fast.

Louis leaned against Avery, knowing they needed to move before somebody strained something; his shoulder was already giving him twinges. But he didn't want to let go.

Finally Avery moved, kissing his cheek and pushing gently at his chest. "Lou, honey, I'm getting squashed."

"Sorry, babe." It took a heck of a lot of effort on the part of his sore thigh muscles to move and his knees felt like raw hamburger. "Damn, I'm too old for this."

Avery laughed, nodding, looking debauched with his fly open and come smeared all over him. "I hear you. Hell, I'm going to have to sneak in to Mama's and change so she doesn't see me looking like this."

"Yeah. It's a good look for you."

"God, Lou." Avery sounded like he could go again and Louis probably could, too, but he was already sore, and uncomfortable, and he was damned amazed at himself, not sure what had just happened. Not sure at all.

"I. We need to. I think I need to sleep on this, Ave."

Slowly, careful of the zipper, Ave sat up, and there was sympathy as well as understanding in Avery's eyes as he zipped up and nodded. "I think that's a good idea. But don't let it make you crazy, Lou. I think we're on the right track."

God, he hoped so.

"Goodnight, Ave."

He got one last warm kiss before Avery slid out of the car, looking like he'd just made out for hours, which wasn't too far off. "Night, Lou."

Avery left without a backward glance, but Lou didn't take that as a bad sign. He decided Ave was right. No over-thinking it. He would just take that as a sign of Avery's confidence that they were doing it right.

And go home and take a fucking shower.

***

The next day passed in a fog for Avery. He planted petunias where he was supposed to be putting phlox. He over-watered Mrs. Bunion's tomato plants and ended up having to buy new and plant them all over again. He just wasn't thinking about work. He was thinking about Lou's mouth on his and Lou's spunk on his skin and about how he wanted to go right over to Lou's that night and do it right, with a bed, and no clothes.

So naturally that was when he ran into Gordon while he was on his way out of Underwood Nursery with an armload of peat moss and a bag of manure. Perfect.

"Why Avery. Up to your neck in shit. How droll."

Avery just gritted his teeth, smiling through them as cheerfully as he could manage. "How delicate of you. How are you, Gordon?"

"Fine. Avery, I would like you to meet Benjamin. Benjamin, Avery."

He hadn't even noticed Gordon was with someone. Avery set his stuff down so his hands could be free to shake, and almost dropped his teeth when he saw who Gordon was with. "Well, Hey, Ben."

"Avery. I didn't know you and Gordon were friends."

"We're not."

Gordon's tone was clipped, harsh, and Avery turned to stare at him. All of his years of practicing his mama's reproving glower must have paid off, because Gordon looked abashed, the tips of those well-shaped ears going red.

"We've known each other a bit. How are you, Ben?"

Ben. Damn, how long had it been since Avery had seen him? Probably almost two years. Their friendship had only lasted so long after Avery had moved in with Louis, as Ben found Lou crass and uncultured, his own words. Avery had told Ben to go to Hell, and since he'd never seen Ben again, had assumed Ben had done just that.

"Oh, just fine." Ben slid one hand into the crook of Gordon's arm, a move so suave and yet so possessive he might as well have lifted his leg and pissed all over Gordon's immaculate pleated trousers. "Gordon is wonderful, isn't he?"

"Oh. Sure." Non-committal was what he strove for. He managed less than completely sarcastic, repressing his snort.

"Are you and Louis still an item?"

"Yes." He gave the answer definitely, unequivocally, and saw Gordon flinch with it. He was sorry for it, as it wasn't his way to be nasty, but as far as he was concerned it was the truth.

"Well. I hope you're as happy with him as I am with Gordon."

Avery nodded slowly, a smile winning the war with wide-eyed disbelief. "I'm sure you

and Gordon will be perfect for each other, Ben.
I wish you the best of luck."

***

"We should go to a Braves game."

Lou looked at Avery from under his lashes,
trying to see what effect his words would have.
He'd never asked Avery to a baseball game
before, knowing that Avery wasn't overly fond
of the game, and figuring the minor league
Greenville Braves would be the last team Ave
would want to see if he did go. Still, spring
training was over and Kyle had tickets he'd
gotten on a student pass, and he'd asked Lou to
ask Avery.

Avery blinked, then smiled hugely, making
him blink in return. "You want me to go?"

"Yeah. So does Kyle."

"Oh."

Avery's face fell and Louis stifled a sigh.
"Kyle and I aren't, you know, doing it
anymore, Ave. We haven't been since you and
I really started dating again. But we're friends
and I think you'd like him, if you give it half a
chance."

He watched Ave push the last bits of lo
mien around on his plate, those rough, chapped
hands he was learning to love, now that Ave
was a real working man too, moving restlessly.

"I just think it would be weird."

"Okay. He and I are going Wednesday night, though, so don't expect me. He'll be disappointed you aren't coming. He bought you a ticket and all."

"Oh. Well."

Man, it was nasty of him to play to Avery's born and bred sense of social correctness, but that was exactly what Lou was doing. Beating Avery down with his own inner Miss Manners.

"So, you'll come?"

"Yes."

He grinned and popped the rest of his egg roll, the hot mustard making his eyes sting. "Cool. I'll pick you up at six."

***

Kyle was a hoot. And a flirt at that, brushing against Avery at every opportunity, making him blush. Lou just looked bemused, a little embarrassed, and a lot horny. It was odd, just like Avery had thought it would be, but it wasn't a bad odd.

In fact, when Louis gave in and made a bathroom run after the second beer, it was odd enough in the good way to set Avery's mind at ease about where Kyle stood.

The kid just turned to him, blunt as anything, and said, "He really loves you, you know?"

"I. Yeah. I know. We're working on it."

"I know." Kyle bounced, cheeks wide with his grin. "He's really hot. You're a lucky guy."

"I'm sorry if…"

"Nah. No need to be sorry. He's been good to me. Now," and here the kid got serious. "You be good to him."

"I will."

Kyle nodded and Avery realized he meant it. This time he would be good to Louis and Lou would be good to him. Not that they weren't before, but he had a feeling they were both a lot wiser this time around.

"Cool. And if you ever get the urge to let me play? Call me."

Oh, God. Louis came back from the bathroom right then and Avery didn't want to explain why he had a suddenly hard dick and a laughing Kyle. Luckily, Lou let it go, and damned if Avery didn't drink beer and eat hot dogs and have the time of his life watching Louis watch baseball.

They should have done this together years ago. Avery was damned grateful that they were getting the opportunity to do it now.

***

"So. That was fun."

They sat in Louis' car, outside Justin's apartment building, and it was full on dark, so Louis figured it was safe to turn toward Avery and lean in for a kiss.

"It was," Avery said against his mouth, lips opening his, tongue pushing in. Louis felt like a teenager, ready to go. He thought maybe Ave was, too, the way the kiss got out of hand so fast, the way Avery moaned into his mouth.

They broke apart who knew how much later, both breathing hard, the soft skin of Avery's throat hot under his palm. "So do you like Kyle?"

"Yeah. He's... he's a good kid. Blunt as Hell."

Louis grinned. "Did he ask about?"

"Yes."

"Hot, huh?"

"Hell, yes."

They kissed again, hard and needy, and Louis knew it was partly just because Kyle had them so revved up, but it was Avery, too, the need for him getting stronger and stronger every time they were together. Louis wanted to beg Avery to come home with him, but he knew that was a bad idea, knew they should wait until classes were over, until more was settled between them, but it was so, so hard, and so was he.

Avery pulled back suddenly, eyes glinting with something dangerous, and then Ave was bending over his lap, braving a beaning on the steering wheel to open Louis' fly and pull out his cock, lips closing around the head and pulling. Louis half shouted, hips rising, almost squashing Avery horribly, but he held back at the last moment, grabbing the wheel and hitting the tilt button so it went all the way up out of the way.

The feeling was unbelievable. Avery sucked him like he knew every hollow, every vein, and Hell, he probably did, even after all this time. Louis just lost his ability to think, completely going with it, moaning and humping and babbling love words. Fuck, it was good, so good, and when Avery touched his balls he came, shooting hard enough that if he didn't have the headrest on his seat, his neck wouldn't have held him up.

The aftershocks took forever to settle and when they did and he could move, he turned, just in time to catch Avery's kiss, tasting himself on the inside of Avery's mouth.

"Let me."

"It's okay, Lou. I sort of creamed my jeans."

"Oh." What the heck could he do but laugh? They were like a pair of teenagers. "Come home with me."

"Oh, Lou." Avery blinked hard, his eyelashes tickling Louis' cheeks. "Next time, okay? You're not ready yet and neither am I."

Louis nodded, chest hurting, but knowing in his gut Avery was right.

"Next time."

Chapter Eleven

Next time turned out to be quite a while in coming and Avery wanted to bash himself in the head every time he remembered turning Louis down.

School was out, both he and Louis having passed with flying colors, amazing considering what all they'd been going through while they did it. Bless his heart, Kyle passed all his classes, too, and they all had a party, drinking way too much beer and flirting too much together, and Avery and Kyle had ended up leaving together because neither Lou nor Kyle were sober enough to get Kyle back home, and he was. Damn it.

After that it was a series of small things. Louis' contractor exams. Avery's rosebush-aphid infestation disaster. Louis' daddy's second car crash in a year.

All of it conspired to keep them, if not apart, at least from getting overly intimate. Avery figured he was just going to explode some day, all over the place like a big balloon or something.

"Avery, honey, are you listening to me?"

He wasn't, not really, and Avery turned to his mama, a little guilty and a lot hot in the face from what he'd been thinking. "Sorry, mama. I was."

"Just thinking of Louis?" She smiled at him, eyes just shining, and she was so happy for him it hurt. She always did like Louis.

"Yeah, mama."

"Well, I knew it wasn't that poor, mangled aloe plant you were blushing over. Though it should be. Just look."

Crap. Sure enough, he'd broken five or six of the waxy stalks right off as he was repotting it. Oh, well. It would do wonders for his skin and maybe when he was jacking off at night, his hand wouldn't catch on his cock so much.

"Avery!"

"What? Oh, sorry. What were you asking?"

"I said, were you going to invite Louis to the Memorial Day cookout?"

"Should I?" He'd thought about it, wasn't sure if it was appropriate.

"Yes, you should. And you should tell him to bring cinnamon rolls."

His mama was a sucker for Louis' cinnamon rolls. It was funny how Louis protested he couldn't cook much, but how they all had a favorite dish. Avery pondered that for a while, thinking back on Gordon's exquisite food and how maybe he liked stew and cinnamon rolls better.

"Okay, mama. But you know his daddy was sick again. He might be going over there for the weekend."

"Well, invite him anyway, honey. Your daddy and I want him to know he's welcome anytime."

"Thanks, Mama." She always made him smile, just by always being herself, damn the torpedoes, full speed ahead. Patting her hand with one of his own dirt smeared ones, Avery nodded. "I'll do that."

***

"Louis? Are you coming over for Memorial Day?"

Louis had bitten the bullet and called his mother, rather than waiting for her to call him. It was such a small thing, but every time he did it she seemed so tickled that he tried to do it more often, just to let her talk. This time he'd called to head her off at the pass on the very thing she was asking him about.

"I have plans for the holiday. But I was thinking I could come take you to church on Sunday. Maybe take you out for dinner after."

"Oh, Louis, that would be grand!" She was just giggling. Goodness.

"I'll see you at the house about nine then."

"Okay, hon. Thank you."

"You're welcome."

"I love you, honey."

"You, too."

They hung up and Louis stared at the phone for a bit, wondering how things had gotten so hard with his mom. Somewhere they had just stopped talking, stopped being on the same wavelength. But they were getting there. It made him happy deep inside.

Almost as happy as being able to call Avery up and tell him, yeah, he could come to the Memorial Day cookout.

***

The Lakewood family cookout was in full swing by the time Avery got there. He was supposed to meet Louis in the parking lot out at Piney Mountain park, but while Louis' car was right there, the man himself was nowhere to be seen.

Damn. Looked like the family had already gotten to him.

Avery was assaulted by his cousin's kids as he walked up to the picnic shelter, going down under a pile of flailing arms and legs and high pitched shrieks of, "Ave! Ave!"

He got untangled who knew how much later, only to get caught by Aunt Blanche, his dad's mama's sister, who wanted to talk to him about her hydrangeas. Bless her heart, she could barely hear him, and she leaned on his arm so heavily he finally got her a lawn chair, and that took another twenty minutes of yes ma'am-in' before he could get away and look for Lou.

Who was standing with Avery's daddy by the grill, both of them wearing aprons and holding beers, doing that manly, communicating without words thing. Lou looked just like he belonged there and Avery felt a big, old sappy wave of emotion come over him, just thrilled as he could be that Louis was back in his life, in whatever capacity, and that they were working toward what passed for normal in their lives again.

"There you are, honey." Avery's mama came around the end of the shelter, holding a baby cousin on one hip. "We saw Louis wandering around in the parking lot and brought him on up with us."

"Thanks, mama."

He saw Louis notice him, saw the smile that popped up just for him, and the happiness just sort of overflowed into his face, stretching his cheeks in a huge grin. His mama was looking from him to Louis and back, grinning hugely herself, and his daddy looked up to see what Louis was looking at, frowning at him.

"You're late. Come on and help us with the hot dogs for all of these hungry heathens."

"Yes, sir." Avery got a pair of tongs and Louis handed him an apron, one of those cheesy kiss the cook ones, but he had a feeling the choice was deliberate, and it made him blush and duck his head, absorbing himself in reaching for a beer.

There was beer and shrimp boil and hot dogs, and Avery and Louis bumped hips and rubbed shoulders and laughed, playing horseshoes with Avery's daddy and volleyball with the teenagers, taking off their shoes and letting the thick grass tickle their feet. They had cherry pie and coffee and sat around listening to the older aunts and uncles talk about who did what to whom way back in the day, fighting off the mosquitoes and holding hands when they were hoping no one was looking.

Even Justin was civil. Avery couldn't have asked for a better day. His heart was light and his belly full and he was getting to spend his first holiday with Louis since the break-up. It just felt so good he thought he might bust.

"It's been a good day."

Avery looked over at Louis, noticing the light in Lou's pretty green eyes, feeling the rough calluses on Lou's thumb as it brushed over the back of his hand. "It's been the best day in a good long while, Lou."

"Yeah." There was a spark in Louis' eyes suddenly, one Avery almost didn't recognize, and the touch of Louis' fingers on his palm became suggestive, a sensual massage.

"How soon can we get away?"

"Uh." Avery floundered, looking around to make sure no one but Louis would notice the color in his cheeks and the twitch in his pants.

"As soon as I can walk without embarrassing myself."

"And how soon is that gonna be?"

Oh, God. Louis was… well, seducing him. That low, gravelly tone of voice took him right back to when they'd met, when he'd flirted with the hot construction worker and gotten way more than he bargained for. This was just the same, his palms getting damp right along with his underwear, his breathing coming quick and hard.

"What are you saying, Lou?" God, help him, he wanted to be absolutely sure. They'd had so many miscommunications.

"I'm saying I want you to come home with me tonight, Ave."

Avery looked down at their joined hands, realizing he held Lou's far too tightly, making white impressions in the tanned skin. He wanted so badly to go home, but he had a feeling. Well, yeah. "Just for tonight?"

Lou nodded, watching him carefully. "It's a start, Ave."

"It is." It was and he could do it, even if the leaving in the morning killed him. "If you're sure? I don't want to rush you, Lou. You have to be ready."

That got him a sharp laugh, a wry look. "I'm ready, babe. I just had to see. I guess I had to convince myself that you still wanted me. Not just that way, but in your life. Being here today, with your family…"

Louis trailed off, but Avery knew, and was amazed at Louis' attempt to even verbalize it. It gave him hope, so big that it swelled his chest with the biggest sigh of relief. "Okay. I'll come home with you. Just give me an ice cube so I can go say goodbye to mama and daddy."

They shared a smile, intimate and warm, and Louis handed him an ice cube out of the nearest cooler so he could drop it right down his pants. That did the trick, making him grimace and dance, wiggling as his cock subsided and the ice melted. His mama almost tried to keep them, patting Louis' arm and telling him how nice it was to see him, but something, maybe the glare Avery shot her way, made her stop so they could leave together, Louis giving him a chaste kiss in the dark before they got in their separate cars to go back to Lou's place.

God, he couldn't wait.

***

Louis sat with his hands glued to the steering wheel, waiting for Avery to catch up and park next to him in the driveway. He was ready. He knew he was. There was no doubt, just nerves. Some little part of him worried that Avery would expect more finesse after being with Gordon, and though Kyle was great in bed, the kid hardly needed finesse, so Lou was out of practice.

Not that Avery had ever really needed finesse, come to that. No, they'd been primal together, hot and dirty and so, so good. Avery was always horny when they first got together, always wanting him. Louis realized he'd taken it for granted, really, and as his shoulder had gotten worse, he'd resented it.

God, he was an idiot.

If he'd had half a brain he would have just told Avery when he was hurting, or too tired, instead of stewing on it.

Headlights flashed in his rearview as Avery turned into the drive, stopping him from stewing about it now. He had more important things to do. Like Ave.

They met at the front door, Ave smiling at him, face and hair a pale blur in the gloom, eyes like holes burned in a blanket. Louis fumbled with the key, hands gone clumsy with the need to hurry, to get inside so he could touch and taste and feel. Yeah, he was so, so ready.

Once inside, Louis turned the lights on, dropped his keys on the table beside the door, then snapped. He grabbed Avery's forearms, pulling Avery close for a kiss, not wanting to break the mood by saying anything stupid and he would if he tried to be suave, or debonair, or whatever. Fuck, Avery tasted good. Like the Fourth of July, even if it was only Memorial Day. Like a picnic with ice cream.

Avery kissed him back, just as hungry, hands coming up to slide over his shoulders and back, little noises coming from Avery's throat. Those noises made Louis crazed. They were like something you didn't even know you'd missed until they popped up again and Louis basked in them and in the feel of Avery's fingers on the back of his neck. The little hairs on Avery's arms caught on Louis' rough fingers, the skin on the inside of Avery's elbows was smooth and hot, and Louis kissed Avery until neither one of them could breathe, until they had to break apart, gasping, staring at each other.

"God, Lou."

"Yeah."

He didn't want to go anywhere with the talking right now, didn't want to fucking second guess anything, so he took Avery's hand and led him to the couch, where they had done so many things so many times, but where it was all new now. They sat, both off balance, falling into each other and laughing. The laughter flowed into their next kiss and before Louis even realized it he was pushing Avery down, searching for more of his taste, more of the feel of Avery's warm body, more of what was dear and familiar and so, so missed.

Avery touched him everywhere, fingers moving over his cheeks and throat, down his arms, over his hips. When they broke to breathe again, Avery grinned at him, eyes so bright with need.

"Want to feel you, Lou. Want skin."

Oh. Yeah. Lou wanted that, too. Wanted everything. He sat up, pulling off his shirt before reaching for Ave's. His hands got tangled with Avery's as Ave reached for him, too. Somehow or another Avery won, slapping his hands away and touching him, stroking the muscles of his belly.

"God. I've missed this six-pack, Lou."

"Yeah?" He grinned, flexed a little.

"Yeah."

They laughed a little more, Avery's fingers digging into his ribs, but it got serious again the minute Avery pinched Lou's nipples. Louis gasped, feeling them tighten, feeling his skin tingle. Ave knew, just like he always knew, and leaned up to lick at one, straining to get to him, and Louis groaned, his cock throbbing in his suddenly tight pants. He broke Ave's hold as soon as he could stand to and struggled with Ave's shirt, lifting Ave up so he could get underneath and pull it off. The skin of Avery's throat tempted him, and Lou pressed his lips there, licking away the salt and suntan lotion taste before sucking hard enough to leave a hickey. God, he wanted Avery to know, to look in the fucking mirror and see it tomorrow, Louis' claim. His 'this is mine' declaration.

Ave moaned, hands scrabbling for purchase, trying to pull him close, but Louis resisted, pushing Avery back again and shifting away so he could get to Ave's jeans, struggling with the button and zipper, petting the little line of dark blonde hair that appeared when he finally got them open. Then Ave's cock was in his hand and the deep, rich scent of Avery was in his nose, and Louis didn't know whether to cry or swear or just burst into tiny bits.

"Lou. I wanted… oh. I need."

He knew exactly what Ave meant. He'd wanted a slow, sweet loving, too, something grand and perfect, but it wasn't going to happen right at the moment, not the way he was humping air and licking his lips over Avery's hardness. He stroked, tightening his grip, and Avery cried out, legs spreading wide, hips pushing up and up.

"We'll have it after this, Ave." It was a promise. After they got the first urgency out, they would learn each other again, and slowly. But now? Now he had to.

Louis bent, taking the head of Avery's cock in his mouth and sucking. Avery let out a sound just short of shrill, whole body shaking, and came right then and there, surprising him, but it was good. So good, having Avery like that. Avery. Not anyone else.

"Oh. Lou."

Licking Avery clean, eyes coming up to meet Avery's shining ones, Louis reared back and unzipped, grabbing his own cock and stroking. Avery just watched him, dazed, eyes wide, as he stroked off quick and hard. His breath came in pants, straining in his chest, and it took pretty much no time for him to come all over his belly and chest, all over Avery's still jean-clad thighs. He thought it might just kill him.

They sat, blinking at each other for a bit, Avery absently rubbing Louis' come into his skin, which was just sexy as Hell. The silence between them became fragile, not tense, exactly, but not something either was ready to break first. Like if they talked it would ruin it.

Which was damned silly. Louis finally got up, knees and back creaking as he hoisted his pants back up. He held out his hand.

"Come to bed with me, Ave?"

Avery smiled, the silence shattered to show them the light beneath. "I thought you'd never ask."

***

They went to their bedroom, because even though Avery had moved out it was still theirs, still the same, and Avery spared a fleeting thought to hoping the sheets had been changed since Kyle had been in them, but then pushed the thought away. He wasn't any better, taking up with Gordon like he had, and at least Kyle was nice, right?

The sheets looked pretty clean when Lou pulled the comforter back and apparently he was being pretty obvious because Lou grinned at him and whapped his arm.

"I changed them this morning. I kinda hoped..."

God, Lou was cute when he blushed like that. Avery nodded. "I hoped so, too. Really, Lou, the place looks great. It's just."

"Old habits die hard."

He laughed, his moment of insecurity fading. "Something like that."

Lou squeezed his hand. "Works for me."

"Oh, good."

They kind of stood there, staring, then each of them made a move for the bed, but heading toward opposite sides, so they sort of stretched their arms and rolled back together. Avery lost it, laughing hard and pushing Louis back on the bed. Lou landed on his back, grunting, and Avery took advantage of it to finish stripping them both. Holy moly, he loved Lou 's body.

Louis just looked at him, green eyes so bright, fevered. "Oh, man, Ave. You... wow. Camera."

"No. I want to look some more." It was like everything snapped back into place, like they were doing it like they used to when it was all new. Louis loved for him to talk, to get down and dirty, as Lou called it. To be eager, take control. He loved it, too, and when he thought about Gordon's perfect, practiced lovemaking he wondered why he'd thought it was a good thing.

"Ave."

"Yeah. Look at you. Getting hard for me again. I want to fuck you, Lou."

"God. Fuck, yeah."

Louis was just begging him with those eyes, with every move of those hips. Avery took pity on them both, because heck, his own cock was growing again, too, just from looking, and he needed to touch. He started with Lou's now bare feet, watching them twitch as he touched the soles, knowing Louis was horribly ticklish. That eased the growing urgency, making Louis snort and flail, making Avery chuckle.

Then it was up Louis' legs, over the short, rough hair, around to the backs of Louis' knees where the skin was baby fine. Avery ran his thumbs up the insides of Louis' thighs, watching Lou twitch and moan before skipping up to his belly to pet, feeling those muscles he loved quiver under his hands.

"You remember the first time I did you, instead of the other way around?"

Louis eyes went from hot green to almost black, a dark flush coming to those cheeks. It was hot as anything. "Yeah. I... I couldn't look at you. Made you do me on my knees. I was fucking scared to death."

"I know." Lou was usually the one doing the doing and when Avery had fucked him the first time? Oh, God, Lou had been tight, hot. "Can we do that again?"

"Hell, yes."

Lou sat up, pulling him in for a kiss that curled his toes, a kiss that said all sorts of things he'd think about later, but for now Avery would just take it, feeling his lips swell from the pressure, feeling the rough burn of Louis' end of the day stubble. They kissed for a long time, both of them touching, just reveling in being able to, and Avery was almost disappointed when Louis finally gave him one last kiss and turned, going up on all fours and presenting that tight, muscled ass. Almost.

"Did your hoping extend to condoms and lube, Lou?"

"In the drawer."

Louis really had been thinking ahead, because there was a brand new tube of lube and a new box of condoms and Avery didn't have to think about who else Lou might have been doing this with. Much.

He took one of the little foil packets out and opened the lube, getting two of his fingers good and slick before turning back to Louis. Oh, was Louis beautiful. Strong back, tight butt, even the tiny scars from Louis' shoulder surgery appealed to him. So hot. Louis was so hard for him, cock bobbing between spread thighs, and Avery was hard, too, aching with the need to be inside Louis, to reclaim him. So he didn't stall anymore, just circled Louis' hole with his fingers, feeling Lou shake, feeling that tight ring of muscle open for him, letting him slide his fingers right in.

A harsh moan came from Louis, his head falling forward between his shoulders.

"Been so long, Ave."

"Am I hurting you?"

"No. Ohsogood. Real good."

It was, too. Louis was so tight around his fingers, so hot, and it was all he could do to take his time and prepare Lou carefully, but Avery had no intention of making this painful. He wanted them both to enjoy it, wanted to make it so good that they would do it again and again.

When Lou was open, panting and begging, Avery slipped his fingers out and grabbed the condom, cursing himself for not putting it on before his fingers got all wet. Still, he managed, because Louis was waiting for him and Avery was so ready. He smoothed the condom on and moved right up behind Lou, pressing against that sweet hole, pushing in slow and easy.

"Ave. Oh. Fuck."

"Yeah, Lou."

"Babe. I. Oh, I need you to move."

"I will, Lou. Hold still a minute."

Avery put a hand on Louis' belly, holding him still, pulling him back tight so he could slide all the way in, hips against Lou's ass, every nerve ending on fire. Lou was tight around him, so tight, tighter than he remembered, and it made him gasp, made Lou grunt.

"Now I can move."

The chuckle he got in response was more of a rasp. "Oh, good."

They moved together. Like they were perfectly timed, Avery pushed in and Lou pushed back, and they got a rhythm going that was way too fast for two guys that had already come once, but it suited them, suited Avery right down to the ground. He leaned forward, over Louis ' back, whispering love words in Lou's ear, letting those strong, workingman's arms hold their weight. Lou rocked back against him, back arching, skin flushed, and Avery slid his hands down Louis' arms, hands covering Lou's where they were planted on the bed, twining their fingers.

"Babe. Just like that time."

Yeah. Just like the very first time they'd done it this way, when he couldn't see Louis' face, but had felt their connection like a live wire through their joined hands and joined bodies.

"Love you, Louis."

Louis cried out, whole body shaking beneath Avery's, hands clenching under Ave's fingers, and just like that Avery felt Louis come, felt the contractions of that incredible body around him, Louis going off without even a touch to his cock.

It was too much. Too much to take without coming, too, and Avery shot hard, fireworks going off behind his eyelids, fingers digging into Louis' hands.

They rested, Avery slipping out when he could and tying off the condom. They were a mess, but he really didn't care. He wanted them to smell like sex. Wanted them to smell like each other. Louis' breathing evened out and he knew Lou was about to doze off, so Avery just curled close, smiling to himself, and was surprised when Louis spoke.

"Love you, too, Ave. Stay?"

"Yeah. I will."

"Good."

He'd stay. At least for the night. And they could both go from there.

Chapter Twelve

The next morning came way too early for Louis. He wanted the fucking sun to go away and give him a few more hours with Avery sleeping at his side, but it wasn't going to happen. He had to get up and go to work. Ave could probably set his own hours these days, but Louis was still on the clock.

He rolled out of bed, leaving Avery muttering, and went to grab a shower. If he invited Ave to join him he'd never leave and that would be bad. Well, it would be good, but bad. He came back out, got dressed, and stuck a granola bar in his mouth, walking back into the bedroom to see Ave sitting up, all naked and warm and blinking.

God, it was hot.

"Hey. I need to go to work." Louis bent, kissed Avery hard before leaning back and oh so casually handing Avery a key. "You can lock up on your way out. And, you know, let yourself in whenever."

Avery grabbed him before he could get away, holding his arm and looking him in the eye. "Are you sure?"

"Yeah. Yeah, Ave. I am."

"Oh. Good." Those amber eyes lit up and Avery pulled him down for one more kiss, happy and sweet. "See you later then."

"Okay, babe. See you then."

He left before he could do any more kissing, or maybe bounce off the walls like a ping pong ball. It wasn't like he had asked Avery to move in or anything. He'd just given Ave his key back. But it felt good, so good that he drove all the way in to work smiling, even stopped and got doughnuts for the whole crew at Winn Dixie because the Krispy Kreme was out of his way. They'd live.

Even Louis' boss noticed his good mood and mentioned it around a mouthful of apple fritter.

"You get some last night, Lou?"

Louis just grinned and nodded. "You sure you really want to know, boss?"

"No. No, I don't. Lalalala, I have no knowledge of it."

"I thought so."

His boss left him alone after that, but the guys didn't, ribbing him all through the day about the spring in his step and the smile on his face. Louis took it all in good humor, too, because every time they ribbed him he thought about Ave and that was a very good way to spend the day indeed.

***

It was all he could do not to rush out and get his toothbrush and his comb and set up shop in Lou's place, because it felt like being home again, and the key in his hand opened up a whole world of possibility as well as Louis' front door.

But Avery didn't. They were taking it slow still and he thought he might just wait until Louis invited him to bring some stuff over before he did. Looking back at their mad rush to be living together the first time, Avery could see his fault in it, could see that he pushed Louis to let him bring his shaving kit, or his work clothes, and that alone had contributed to their not getting to know how the other lived, to not knowing what sorts of troubles they might have meshing lifestyles.

He needed to get to work, too, though his first consultation wasn't until ten. Still, a shower, shave, and change of clothes was in order before he met with his magnolia and evergreen lady. Locking up carefully, Avery headed out, trying to think what he should do next. Not with work, he knew that, but with Louis. Should he come back that night? Or should he call? Would it seem like he was pushing if he did? Would it seem like he was panicking if he didn't?

Finally he decided he would call and that would be that. They'd just have to go from there. Avery spent the rest of the day caught up in bug identification and moss removal and tried not to over-think things. That would cause nothing but trouble. And when he felt like he'd let enough time pass, he called Louis on his cell.

"'Lo?"

'Hey, Lou. I was wondering…"

"Ave! Hey." Oh. Louis sounded happy to hear from him, voice warm and deep and full of anticipation.

"Hey. I was wondering. Would you like to have dinner? I could pick something up. Bring it to your place. Maybe some fried chicken and cole slaw?"

"Stop at Bi Lo and get me a coconut cream pie and you're on."

"Can do." Avery grinned, staring at nothing. "I'll see you after work, then?"

"You bet."

"Okay. Later."

"Bye."

Well, that went about as well as he could have wished for. Avery did a little elbow pump before going to finish his paperwork for the day so he could get out of there and run to the store to pick up dinner and go home. Even if it wasn't officially his home again yet.

*   *   *

Hearing from Ave was the best part of a fucking long day. Lou was pooped, but he hadn't wanted to tell Avery that, hadn't wanted to ruin the fragile, new thing they had. Well, that and he was still riding the euphoria from the night before.

But after a holiday he and the crew had worked double time and Lou had filled in more than he should have, strictly, and his whole body throbbed in the not so good way. Maybe he had time for a shower before Avery got there.

Of course, about the time he thought that, Avery knocked on the door. Louis sighed, summoning a smile from somewhere deep, and opened up.

"Hey, Ave. You have a key."

"Yeah, but I have my hands full."

Louis thought it was maybe more than that, but he let it go, grabbing the bag Avery held out to him. "You even brought beer."

"Yeah. I thought you might could use one."

"Thanks."

Lou made a break for the kitchen, some nameless, nagging thing putting a knot in his belly. He wanted to see Ave. He did. Heck, he was happy Avery was there with dinner so he didn't have to scrounge up the energy to make something, or call and order pizza. But he was so damned tired. He was leaning on the counter by the sink, elbows locked and head down when he felt Avery's hand on his back.

"Lou? Are you... you look bushed."

"I am." What was he thinking the other day? That he should have just told Ave when he was tired and hurting? Well, here was his chance. "I'm sorry, babe, I just… it was a long day and I'm pooped."

"Yeah." He got a kiss on the cheek and then Avery was moving about the kitchen, pulling out plates and cups and getting out his iced tea pitcher. "Why don't you go take a shower while I get dinner ready? Some hot water ought to help."

Louis looked over, expecting Ave to be looking anywhere but at him, hiding disappointment in a thin mouth and hunched shoulders like he used to, but Ave was staring right at him, concern easily discernable in Avery's eyes.

"Yeah. Yeah, I think I will. Thanks, Ave."

"No stress, hon."

The hot water did feel good pouring down on his shoulders and neck, releasing a day's worth of hard work and tension. And to his amazement, Louis didn't feel the need to rush out there and be with Avery. Or maybe the better word was to entertain Avery. Like he was a host with the most or some shit. No, it was like Avery belonged there, maybe more than he had the first time, because Louis didn't feel the pressure to be with him even though he was in the house.

When he was finally out and dry and dressed in some soft sweats and a t-shirt, Louis headed back out, smiling when Avery handed him a beer. "Thanks."

"Sure. You want to eat on the couch?"

"Oh, that sounds great."

The coffee table was already set up and Louis groaned as he sat, never more grateful for his couch than at that moment. The food looked great. So did his living room.

"You tidied up."

Ave's laugh was purely rueful. "Reflex, Lou. Not criticism."

He decided to believe that and nodded. "It's been neater since Kyle stopped coming over. That kid was a slob."

Avery gave him a look, eyes just laughing at him. "You don't say."

"Hell, yes." Lou was grinning himself, feeling a hundred percent better as he grabbed a chicken leg and some potato salad. "I was always tripping over his shit."

"Imagine that."

"It's different when it's not your stuff. I get that now."

Avery didn't say anything, just waggled an eyebrow, and they ate in companionable silence, Louis polishing off three pieces of chicken and two beers, and yawing his way through the news when Avery turned it on. Ave cleaned up the dishes and came back to sit with him and he was plain just nodding off in no time.

"Camera."

"Huh?"

Avery grabbed his hand, tugging him down. "Take a nap. Even just a short one will do you some good."

"Oh. 'Kay." That sounded like such a good idea that Louis settled across Avery's legs and did just that. He was asleep in no time.

***

Louis woke up with kind of a stiff neck, but feeling a huge amount better than he had. How many hours ago? He squinted at the TV and found that it was on some sitcom, so it couldn't have been that long. Grunting, he levered himself up off Avery's legs.

"How long was I out?"

"About an hour."

"Did I snore?"

"A little." Didn't look like Ave minded, in fact Avery had this look, sort of a fuzzy, sentimental look. "You were cute. You drooled."

He checked the sides of his mouth for dried drool and whapped Avery's thigh when there was none. "Liar."

"Made you look."

"Uh huh." Oh, man, suddenly he had to piss. Two beers and a big old glass of iced tea were making themselves known, so he hopped up and made a run for it, Avery's laughter trailing behind. When he came back out, he gave Ave a baleful glare. "You are a cruel man."

"Keep it up and I won't give you pie."

"Ooh. Pie." Lou stood in front of Ave, hands on his hips. "What do I have to do for pie?"

"Oh, I dunno. Give me a kiss?"

That he could do and Louis bent to press his lips to Avery's, loving how smooth and hot Avery's mouth was under his. They kissed long and deep and he was really getting into it until Avery's hands came up, grabbing his shoulders, one of them pressing right into a sore spot on his bad arm. Louis hissed and jerked back and Avery grimaced.

"Oh, jeez, Lou. I'm sorry."

"S'okay, Ave." Part of him wanted to shrug it off and be all manly and go on and do the deed, even though he was hurting. The other part, the sensible one, told him that was what he'd done before and was what had caused part of their trouble. Better to be honest. "I'm sorry, Ave. I don't think I'm up to hanky panky tonight. I hurt."

"You don't have to apologize, Louis." Avery sounded just like Avery's mama. Gently chiding, but concerned. It made him smile.

"Well, I am up to pie. And maybe some Scrabble?"

"Oh!" Ave looked so pleased that Louis decided to believe that he didn't need to say he was sorry anymore over the lost opportunity to neck. "That would be great. Some decaf, too?"

"Sure."

Watching Avery get up and bustle about to make coffee and set the Scrabble board up and cut them some pie made him happy in his bones. So did knowing he had the guts to speak up for what he wanted. And that Ave would listen when he did.

They? Were getting there.

***

Avery got back to the apartment early, having put Louis to bed and saying he ought to go home so Lou could sleep. Not because he didn't want to stay. More like he was afraid that if he did, he'd push Louis into having sex and he didn't want to do that when Lou wasn't feeling well. Thank God Lou had taken it as he meant it and not thought of it as punishment.

He let himself in, surprised to find that Justin was already home. His brother had been spending a lot more time away lately, coming in during the wee hours of the morning.

"Oh, hey Avery. You're back. Good. I uh, need to talk to you."

Justin's ears were red and he wouldn't quite look at Avery, which was always a bad sign.

"What's up?"

"I. Well." Justin finally looked up, face red, grimace plain. "I kinda need you to move out."

"Kinda?" Avery almost smiled, but managed not to. No doubt this whole thing was hard for Justin. Bless his little pointed head.

"Yeah. I mean I do. I um, asked my girlfriend to move in with me."

"You did?" Wow. "Cool! That's great, Just. You must really like her."

"I do." Now Justin was grinning, meeting his eyes confidently, obviously feeling good about his subject. "I think... well, I think I'm in love with her, Ave. She's just the sweetest and the prettiest and I really like being with her."

Avery thought about hugging Justin, but figured it would be awkward, so he patted Just's arm instead. "That's great, man. I can stay with Mama and Daddy for a bit if... well, I can stay with them."

That got him a look. "You dumped the Gordon guy, right? If you're thinking about moving in with anyone it's Louis again?"

"Yeah." Oh, God, the thought made him almost dizzy. To live with Lou again full time. "When do you need me out?"

"Well her lease is up in two months. So no later than then."

"I can do that."

"Oh." Justin just beamed at him, looking happier than he had since Avery had moved in. "You rock. And besides, living with you has really prepared me for living with a girl."

Avery snorted. "Gee. Thanks."

***

"Hey, Avery honey. Would you like some iced tea?"

Avery grinned at his mama, hugging her neck and kissing her cheek before going to get the tea. "You sit, momma. I'll get it and get you some, too."

"My, you're in a good mood."

"I am. Justin is kicking me out."

He turned back with the tea just in time to see her wrinkle her brow at him. "Well, darlin', if you think that' s good."

"Oh, he didn't tell you?" He hoped he wasn't stepping on Justin's toes.

"Tell me what? Hand me the lemon will you, honey?"

The lemon juice stung his fingers as he handed it over. "Well, his girl is moving in as soon as her lease is up."

"Really?" His mama clapped her hands, beaming at him. "Oh, I like her. She'll keep him in line. She's just what he needs."

"Yeah. She's just right."

"So, where are you going?" She sipped her tea, looking at him over the rim of the glass. Waiting. Watching him like a hawk.

"I was thinking I could stay here a bit, if I have to."

"Well, of course you can, sweetie. I was just hoping."

"Mama, you are transparent as glass. I don't know if Lou and I are ready for that. I wish we were, and maybe in two months we will be, but I pushed it last time and it went bad. I don't want to this time."

That was the flat truth. They needed to know it was right, not just get swept along in the heat of the moment. Avery thought it was going so well. Why, look how Louis had talked to him the other night, telling him he was too tired instead of doing what Avery wanted and resenting it. And instead of taking it as some kind of proof Louis didn't want him, Avery had worked hard to take it in stride and at face value, accepting that Louis was too tired. He didn't want to ruin that kind of progress with pushing too hard.

"Okay, honey." His mama just smiled. "I just liked so much seeing y'all together at the cook out. Made my heart glad."

Avery succumbed to the urge to just get up and hug her silly. How many other Southern mamas would give their blessing like that to their son and another man? She hugged him back just as hard, and he thought maybe she knew why because she whispered in his ear, "I just want you to be happy."

"I will be, mama. I promise."

***

"Let's go out to dinner."

Louis looked up at Avery from where he sat on the floor putting the new bookcase he'd gotten together. "Where? " It was a lazy Saturday evening and Louis wasn't sure he was inclined to go out, but for the right food, he would.

"Smokin' Stokes."

"Oh." Ouch. Louis loved that place, with their Cheerwine barbeque sauce. It didn't get any better than that. He dropped his hex driver. "Just let me clean up and we'll go."

He stood, heading for the shower, because he'd been working around the house all day while Ave worked in the yard, muttering about his weeds. Didn't take him long to realize Ave was following him.

"You want something?"

"Yeah." Ave's hand slid along his back and down to his ass to pat. "A shower. And to cop a feel or two. We might as well share water."

"Oh." Well, that was a good idea. Lou grinned. "There you go. Come on then."

Taking a shower with Avery was a luxury he'd forgotten. Probably for his own good, when he was alone. And with Kyle, if they bothered, it was a quick scrub and jack. Nothing like the sensual experience it was with Ave.

"You still buy the soap I like."

They were in the shower, water falling on them, and Louis turned to face the spray, hiding his hot face. "Yeah, I like the way it smells."

"Me, too."

He jumped when Avery's soapy hands found his back, moaned when they started massaging the suds into his skin, and he swayed, a wave of love and longing and, yeah fear, washing over him. If he got used to this again and lost it. Well, he'd have to fight harder this time. And maybe not tell Avery to leave.

The sweet touches continued, Avery finally turning him gently, hair wet, skin shining with soap. Louis bent and kissed Ave, hand coming up to cup the back of Avery's neck, tilting Avery so Louis could push his tongue between those soft lips and taste. So good. So fucking hot. He was hard, so hard, and it was fast enough to make him a little dizzy, that southward rush of blood.

"Babe. Love you."

"Yeah, Lou. You, too."

Avery was hard against him, too, pushing that long cock against his hip, making him want things they really couldn't do standing up in a slippery shower. So instead Louis scooped up some of the slick soap and grabbed Avery's cock, making Avery gasp and move close, closer, trying to crawl right into his skin. Louis pumped gently, then harder, his own prick pushing into Avery's waiting hand, and the circle of pleasure completed itself, shorting out his brain.

They rocked and slid, hips moving, feet planted precariously on the tile, gasping. The water was its own kind of caress, sensitizing them, making Louis want to shout with how good it was. Chill bumps rose on his skin, his nipples growing tight enough to hurt, his cock on fire, and finally Louis couldn't take it any more. He came hard, seeing stars, his spunk washing down over Avery's wrist to the drain.

Close behind, Avery jerked against him, cock pulsing in Louis' grasp, grunting and swaying as he came, so damned pretty in his passion that Louis wanted to see that look again and again.

"Well." Avery leaned against him, whooping for breath. "We're all clean."

"We are. Don't you poop out on me. You promised me barbeque."

"I did." That smile was almost better than Avery's face when he came. Almost. "Let's get dried off and go then."

"You know it."

***

Smokin' Stokes was crowded and noisy, but Avery didn't care, not with Louis looking like that, all happy and relaxed, wet hair reminding him what they'd been doing not too long before. He'd always loved Louis right out of the shower, the lemon and pine scent of the soap he'd bought for Lou once on a whim so dear and familiar it made his chest ache. In a good way.

They got seated, ordered up some pork with Cheerwine sauce and some bbq baked potatoes and started in on the bread, grinning at each other and dipping it into sauce. Talking about everything and nothing. It was so good, so relaxed and easy.

Which was, of course, when something made Louis stiffen up and look really upset. Avery looked over his shoulder and damned if there wasn't the last person he would ever have expected to see in a smokehouse.

"Well, hello Avery."

"Hello, Gordon. This isn't the sort of place I would expect you to like." His even tone was hard won, but it was better to let both Gordon and Louis think he was perfectly okay with this, and damn it, he should be. He'd broken up with Gordon, sure, but he wasn't the one who'd been a bitch about it.

"We're slumming."

There man with Gordon was the same one that Avery had seen him with at the nursery that day. Ben. Avery smiled tightly at him.

"Ben. Hi. You remember Louis."

"Of course. Louis." The tilt of Ben's nose said more than even the tone of his voice what he thought of Louis and Avery tried not to get up and punch him right on it.

"Ben." Louis was just as short, if not more so, but to his credit, he said nothing more.

"Congratulate me, Avery. Ben has consented to move in with me."

"Really?" It came out a bit more dry than he wanted it to, but Avery couldn't help it. The poor guy had to be at least as uptight as Gordon then. Not to mention that saying something like that was totally inappropriate when you were just introducing someone and Gordon could only be doing it to try to hurt him. Avery smiled brightly. "Congratulations! I hope your life with each other is perfect."

"What about you two. Have you moved in together again?" Gordon looked at Ben, smile turning vicious. "Isn't it sweet, the story behind these two? On again, off again."

"I'm not sure if that's any of your business."

Louis' voice was low, almost ominous, and Avery couldn't have been happier for their food to arrive, because it gave him an excuse to nod and smile and say, "Well, it was good to see you, Gordon. You too, Ben," and look to their food, dismissing the other couple. Gordon got the hint, pulling Ben away, and Louis made a disgusted noise.

"Well, that didn't take him any time."

Avery just laughed. "He was ready to settle down, I think. That's the only reason I can think of that he asked me to move in, because really, we were so not right for each other."

"Good."

"Don't let him get to you, babe." Avery paused, not sure if this was the right time, but seeing it as an opening. "He did remind me there was something I was going to tell you, though. Justin is kicking me out at the end of next month and I'll be moving in with Mama and Daddy for a bit. Just until I figure out what kind of place I want."

There. That sounded decisive and casual. Not a hint of 'I'm waiting for you to ask me to move back in.'

"Yeah?" Louis was looking at him, non-committal, waiting for him to go on. "What's with him?"

"His girlfriend is moving in."

"Well I'll be damned."

"That's what I said. Anyway, I thought you ought to know."

"Cool."

The disappointment needed to be pushed aside. He'd said himself they didn't need to rush things and he wasn't expecting some kind of declaration or offer, he'd just wanted to tell Louis before anyone else did. If it hurt a little that Lou was so cavalier about it; that was his own problem.

Avery changed the subject, chattering brightly about his old lady clients and the terrible aphids and how he was going to have to study up more on roses because they had never really been his strong suit, munching his barbeque and trying to keep from thinking too much. After he'd repeated himself about the fifth time, though, Louis took one of Avery's hands in his, stilling him.

"Ave, I wish I could just ask you to move back in, but I'm not sure we're ready, either of us."

"I know." He did. He really did. It was just so hard. "I want you to. I want to. But at the same time I know we need to keep from rushing it and if you asked me now it would be for the wrong reasons. I wasn't hinting, I just thought I ought to tell you and not let you hear it later and think I was skulking around until you did ask."

"I won't. Think that, I mean. I just need…"

"Time. Yeah, I know." Avery squeezed Louis' hand, chest loosening up. "I can wait."

"Good. Now eat up. I want some pecan pie."

"Yes, sir."

Chapter Thirteen

The cake was a little lopsided, but he had butter pecan ice cream and a really neat looking planter with a creeping Charlie in it and a big old gift certificate to the local nursery, too. The nice thing about Avery's birthday was that it was right before the Fourth of July, so Louis never really forgot it.

They'd have dinner, then cake and ice cream, and then Louis figured if Avery wanted to, they'd go out dancing. They hadn't gone clubbing since they got back together, which was maybe an attempt on their part to avoid some of their old friends and acquaintances, but he wouldn't have a quarrel with seeing Avery get his groove on, all sweaty and hot and yummy. Nope, not one fucking problem with that.

All he had to do now was to wait for Avery to show up. Louis paced, looking out the front curtain every so often, knowing Avery wasn't anywhere near late, but impatient to get started. He hadn't made Brunswick stew; it was too hot, but he had Avery's favorite cold meal of fancy chicken salad with almonds and celery, with some crusty bread and sweet potato chips all ready, and finally, there was Ave's little SUV.

He opened the door before Avery even got there, taking in how damned good Avery looked in chinos and a white, open collar shirt.

"Hey, babe."

"Hey." Avery pushed right up against him and kissed him, arms sliding around his waist. "You look edible."

"Hungry, huh? Happy birthday, Ave."

"Oh. Thanks." That got him the biggest smile and another kiss, one so enthusiastic he almost forgot about dinner.

"I made chicken salad."

"Wow." They went arm and arm back into the air-conditioned house, Avery leaning against him, body solid and warm. "Mama wants to know if you're coming to the fireworks party day after tomorrow."

"Sure." He had to stop and kiss Avery again, breathing deep to get the scent of Ave's shampoo and the underlying smell of Avery's skin. Avery kissed him back, pushing up against him, hands stroking his shoulders and neck and hair. It had been like that since they started seeing each other again, just like it was when they first started dating. Hot and urgent.

"I'll tell her."

He almost asked, "Tell her what?" but figured it out before he did. Right. Esther. Fireworks. Dinner. Louis dragged Avery to the table, pulling out a chair for him. "You want iced tea or Coke?"

"Iced tea will be fine. You're spoiling me."

"It's fun."

It was fun, too, watching Avery smile and laugh and just be there with him, sharing space and company and all. Louis hummed as he served up dinner, putting out the pickles Avery liked, too, and some lettuce and tomato for the sandwiches.

"I thought we might go dancing later."

"Oh, that sounds good."

That wasn't just Ave being polite, either, Louis could tell from the surprised pleasure in Avery 's eyes. The pleasure doubled when he presented Ave with homemade cake and butter pecan ice cream and presents. The plant got him a kiss and the gift certificate got him a grope. Damn. Nice.

"Thanks so much, Lou. This is the best birthday I could ask for."

"Yeah?"

"Yeah."

"Cool." God, he was stoked. Avery was smiling, touching him every time he got near enough, just looking happy with life, and it made Louis happy, too, deep inside. For that look he'd pick up dirty laundry and wet towels and make lopsided cakes for the rest of his life.

"Move in with me, Ave."

Avery blinked up at him, looking stunned, a smile breaking over that much loved face.

"Are you sure? I could go to Mama and Daddy's, Lou. Really. I don't want you to ask me just because I have to be out of Just's next week."

"I'm not. Asking because of that, I mean." Fuck, he hated trying to put this shit into words, but try he would. For Ave. "I miss you. I mean, I know we spend a lot of time together, but I miss having you here at home. Does that make sense?"

Standing, moving close, Avery cupped Louis' cheek with one hand. "It makes perfect sense, babe, but I want you to be sure." Avery laughed. "I seem to say that a lot lately, but I don't want to go through what we did again, you know?"

"I know." Oh, boy, did he know, and he'd thought hard about it ever since Ave had said he'd have to move out of Justin's, agonized over it in ways he never really did, in fact, and he'd decided that he wanted Avery home. With him.

"I want you here with me."

"Oh, babe." Avery hugged him, kissed his mouth. "I think I need to think about it."

Louis tried to hide the hurt that caused, but he couldn't hide the sudden stiffness of his body, the way his hands dropped from Avery's hips. "Okay."

"No. Don't, Lou, please. It's just... I'm scared. Please. Let's just go out dancing and talk about it a little later, after it's had time to sink in."

Swallowing the words that tried to come up, and his pride, Louis nodded. "Okay. Yeah. I can do that."

"Thanks, Lou." Avery hugged him again, tight enough to make his ribs creak, and kissed his neck, right where it met his jaw. Louis relaxed a little, understanding why Avery might want time to think, because hadn't he just been thinking about how long he'd been thinking about it? Or whatever? He needed to give Avery time. It wasn't a bad thing to be cautious.

"Well, uh. What time do you want to go out?"

"How about nine-ish? The dancing should be good then."

"Right."

Louis felt like a block of wood, standing there, and Avery finally kissed him one more time and shoved him toward the couch. "Go sit. I'll do the dishes and be right there."

Moving automatically, Louis did just that, his mind running in circles until Avery joined him, hands still damp and smelling like Dawn, sitting close to him on the couch and snuggling right up. Avery was a great snuggler.

He woke up about eight thirty, Ave leaning on his good shoulder, breathing deep and even. Damn. He was feeling kinda loggy-headed, but much better about the Avery moving in situation. Avery would say yes. He just wanted to show Louis how committed he was to taking things seriously this time, Louis was sure. He had no doubt things would work out.

He smacked Avery's hip. "Hey. Get up, if you want to go dancing."

"I do." The sound was muffled by Avery's face being squashed against his shoulder, but eventually Avery moved, and they got up, got their clothes straightened out and got on the road. Heading for the Castle, which was not Louis' favorite, but Avery loved it, and it was Avery's birthday, so who was he to say no? Well, he could have, and these days he had reason to believe Avery wouldn't pout about it, which was really cool, but he didn't need to complain. Next time they'd go to someplace more his speed.

The Castle was jumping and there were drink specials galore and Louis grinned as Avery bought them both no more than a Coke before dragging him out on the floor. Oh, cool, it was eighties night. That he could dance to, even if it did take him back to, like, eighth grade when he was still trying to hide the fact that he was watching the boys instead of Suellen Norton, who had declared that she would marry Lou someday and have his babies.

Avery was all over him. Swaying, rubbing, eyes closed as he sang along with the music, and Louis admired him. Fuck, it made him hard when Avery was like that, because it was like having sex, even with their clothes on and a crowd watching. Which sounded kinda... kinky. Song after song they danced, and finally he needed a drink and a piss, and he touched Avery's hip, yelling over the music.

"Need to go. Be right back, okay?"

Nodding, still dancing, Ave gave him a thumbs-up and he headed off. Yeah, he'd like to see Gordon dance with Ave like he did. Louis snorted. He got a drink after hitting the john and caught his breath, sitting on the sidelines a bit and watching Avery go. Until some redheaded kid went up to Avery and started dancing with him like he had a right to touch. Then? Louis got pissed. Even more so when the kid grabbed Avery's hips and rubbed.

Even as Louis charged into the fray Avery was backing off, giving the kid an apology, and Louis barged right between them, giving his own look, which was more of a fucking scowl. The kid grinned and shrugged, heading off, and Lou turned to Avery.

"You know him?"

"We met once. C'mere and dance with me."

Louis went. He'd have to keep a closer eye on Avery. No way was Louis sharing him. No way in Hell.

***

Strangely enough it was Louis' jealousy that made up Avery's mind. They were on their way home, Louis looking at him possessively every now and then, hand coming out to rest on his thigh, petting gently. It thrilled him, much as he probably shouldn't admit it, made his muscles jump under Lou's fingers, made his dick hard as a rock. It was like all of the careful thinking in the world couldn't hold up to the primal feel of Louis declaring him his for the whole world to see. Or at least the folks at the Castle, including poor Ed, who had no reason to think he wasn't still single until Louis almost ripped the kid's head off.

They got back home just in time. Because otherwise Avery was going to explode. Avery grabbed Lou's hand and dragged him right up to the door, pulling out his key and using it for the first time, locking the door back behind him before pushing Louis back against it and kissing him. Hard.

They didn't take their time. They weren't gentle. Like he was still hearing the beat of the music, Avery danced Louis all the way over to the couch and pushed him down on it, straddling him and kissing so hard they both gasped for breath when the kiss was done.

"Jeez, Ave."

"I want you in me, Lou."

"On the floor."

Louis gave him a shove and Avery toppled off on the floor, bouncing off the coffee table and not giving a damn, and Louis slid off and got behind him, yanking at his chinos and pulling them down, pushing him so he bent over the couch, ass in the air.

"Damn it. I need. Hold on." Avery laughed as Louis' weight and heat disappeared and tried to hold onto the mood. Luckily it didn't take Louis long and the urgency came right back as Louis slid two strong, slick fingers along his crease and between his cheeks, nudging his hole. God, yeah, he needed that. Avery pushed up and back, begging for it, and Lou gave, those thick fingers sliding right in and opening him up.

"Tight. Hot. Oh, babe."

"Yeah. Louis, please."

Avery's cock was so hard, so tight, and he needed, and Lou didn't waste much time on preparation thank God, just stretched him good and wide and pulled out, pushing at Avery with that cock instead. The head slid inside and Avery just moaned, loving the feel of it, loving how raw it was. No finesse, just battering lust. Just pure need.

He rocked back and Louis thrust forward and they got a rhythm going, hard and deep and necessary. His knees stung where they scraped the floor, his elbows hurt where they dug into the edge of the couch, and Avery gloried in it. Sweat dripped in his eyes,

stinging like the tears he'd shed when he was
missing this so, only so much better, and
Avery started gasping out love words, letting
Louis know he knew who he was with, letting
Louis know how much he wanted.

Louis grunted, grabbing his hips in a
bruising grip and pounding him, pushing and
pushing, finally reaching around with one hand
for his cock and pumping it. Lou's thumbnail
scraped over Avery's slit, then those fingers
slid down his shaft to his balls, and Avery
cried out, jerking, trying to come, trying not to
so he could wait on Lou, his head spinning.
Louis just kept on, on and on, until finally he
heard a harsh moan, felt Louis' prick jerk
inside him as Louis filled the condom up his
ass, and Avery lost it, a loud, glad shout
escaping him as he shot, his head snapping
back so Louis could kiss him deep and hard, so
they could share breath as the last spasms
rocked them both.

"Lord Almighty, Ave."

Yeah. Summed it up just right. Avery
laughed, unable to move or to hold himself up.
He had the worst case of baby head. He just
laid there, propped up on the couch, sweat
drying on his skin.

"I wanna come home, Lou. Want to move
back in."

"Oh, thank God." Louis kissed his neck,
hand curling around his ribcage to pull him
even closer. "When?"

"This weekend."

"Perfect."

***

It didn't take much to move him back in, really. He had mostly clothes and some small pieces of furniture, a ton of plants and some knick-knacks. Justin helped him, mainly for the free pizza, he thought, but Avery had to laugh when they got there and Louis put Justin, and him, to work.

In a fit of some sort of nesting instinct or something, Louis had cleared our most of the furniture and had drop cloths down so they could paint the living room and the bedroom, and there was a carpet shampooer, too and a thundering herd of college students led by Kyle.

Avery just sort of blinked at Lou over his coffee and Louis laughed at him, kissing him hard enough to take his breath before marshalling the troops and getting everyone to work with promises of some gourmet coffee and hot Krispy Kremes.

By noon they had a tan bedroom with a Myrtle Beach feel to it and a pretty cream with slate trim living room. The pizza had arrived and they were all sitting around munching, with Avery watching fondly as Louis and Kyle essentially beat the snot out of each other. So manly.

"Isn't that weird?"

"Hmm?" Just sat down next to Avery, sucking down a root beer, and Avery looked over at him. "What's weird?"

"Well, Louis and him. Didn't they date or something?"

"They did. For a while after Lou and I broke up. But Lou's with me, now. They're just friends."

"That would freak me out, my girlfriend did that."

"Yeah, well, then I'd start worrying she was a lesbian, if she could take Lou."

"That's not what I meant."

"Are you really getting pissy on my behalf, little brother?"

Justin looked surprised, then sheepish. "I guess I am. I just don't want to see him hurt you anymore."

It warmed him, Justin's concern, but to be fair he had to correct that. "I hurt him, too."

"Yeah, well, much as I like Lou, he's not my brother."

Justin's cheeks flushed a dull red and he wouldn't look at Avery, but it was still probably the nicest thing Justin had ever said to him. He whapped Justin on the knee affectionately. "Thanks."

"Yeah, whatever."

***

They ended up staying in a hotel that night because the paint fumes were so bad they couldn't stand it. Louis hoped to Hell Ave wasn't too disappointed, because when you moved in with someone you expected to stay where you moved.

Still it was like a mini vacation. They had a steak dinner and shared a big old piece of chocolate cake and were changing into their bathing suits to go sit in the hot tub. Louis enjoyed the view as Avery stripped down and put on his trunks, trying not to let himself get over-stimulated before they went out amongst 'em.

"You're not upset, are you?"

"What? No! This is great. We deserve it after working so hard today."

"We do. I just wanted to make sure. I mean, we never had time to be alone all day and now we can't even stay in the house and…"

Avery came over to him and put one hand on his mouth, shutting off his nervous flow of words. Him, who never talked more than he had to.

"It's okay, Lou. This is wonderful. And we have all day tomorrow to potter around the house."

"True. I just wanted everything to be nice. I think I got a little carried away."

"It's the contractor in you."

He had to laugh at that, nodding a little. Houses needed clean walls and carpets, even if he did just throw his wet towels on them. They headed out, both of them slinging towels over their shoulders, and it was late enough that the kiddies had all left the pool and the hot tub was empty. That was a darned good thing. Not that he was going to get freaky in a public hot tub, but he and Ave could flirt and play footsie without bothering anyone.

They moved back and forth between the hot tub and the pool, getting all warm and loose before dipping in the cooler water of the pool, laughing and splashing and talking until the little girl that worked behind the desk came and told them it was time for the pool to close and could they please go away, only much nicer.

Damn, but his legs were rubbery. Louis wobbled and Avery put an arm around him, helping him stay upright.

"You okay, babe?"

"Yeah, I think I just… Maybe I need to go back and sit down."

"You bet."

Wow. He'd spent too much time in the water, he guessed. They got upstairs and Avery stripped him out of his wet suit and put him in his cotton sleep pants, like he was a kid. It made him chuckle, just thinking about how not fatherly Avery was, and about how his grand seduction scene was not working, because he was just going to fall asleep where he sat. Louis yawned.

"Sorry, Ave. I meant this to be such a good day."

"It was." Avery curled up next to him, wet trunks gone, soft boxers in their place. "It was the best. I love you, Lou."

Oh. That was nice to hear. So damned nice. He yawned again, eyes drooping closed. "Love you, too."

"Night, Lou."

"Mmhmm." And with that, he let Avery soothe him right into sleep.

***

The house still smelled like paint when they got home, but only just, the scent having dissipated overnight. The house was hot as the hubs of Hell, though, what with the windows being open, and the first thing Louis did while Avery unpacked the groceries they'd bought was go around and close windows and put the air conditioning on. Lord love refrigerated air.

The bedroom stopped him dead in his tracks, his mouth dropping open at what he saw.

"Ave! Avery, come look at this."

"What?" Ave slid up behind him, arms slipping around his waist.

"Look."

Avery peeked over his shoulder. "Oh, cool. Do you like it?"

Did he? A rich blue, quilted comforter had replaced the faded off white one that had been there before, and cream and blue silk shams gleamed above the top of the turned down, white cotton sheets. There was even a bucket with a champagne bottle and artistically arranged seashells on the bedside table.

"It looks like Trading Spaces was here."

"I gave Justin the spare key and told his girlfriend what I wanted. I thought it fit the theme we did with the new paint and the curtains. I'm glad you didn't paint the bed, though. I missed the green monster."

Louis turned in Avery's embrace, looking right into those sweet eyes. Ave looked so happy and Louis had to kiss the man. Starting off new was a good thing, this would be their new place, not the place they'd shared before, or the lonely bed he'd been in when Ave wasn't there.

"I love it. We should try it out, though. Make sure it's as soft as it looks."

"We should."

That smile got so wide and Avery pulled him close, even closer, giving him a kiss that curled his fucking toes. Damn. At least one of them could manage the grand seduction scene. He pulled Avery with him to the bed, tugging at Ave's clothes, wanting to see Avery naked on that blue comforter, all skin and pale gold hair and need.

"Lou. Need you."

The breathless, deep tone of Avery's voice drove Louis nuts and he finally got Ave's shirt off and his pants down and shoved, making Avery oof as he landed on the bed. Then he could get to Avery's sneakers and socks and yank the jeans and underwear off, too. When Avery was nude Louis stopped and looked, hands clenched into fists to keep from touching, just for a minute.

The shine of Avery's skin rivaled the silk on the pillows and that hair was like spun gold. Poetic maybe, or sappy, but there it was. In contrast Avery's eyes were almost black, hot with need and wanting. Avery held out a hand.

"Come on, babe. I need you."

"Let me get naked."

"Oooh. Put on a show for me, babe."

Oh, Lord. Louis did the best he could, showing off, flexing a little as he took of his shirt and his jeans, hoping he didn't look like the biggest fool on the planet. Looked like Avery liked it, though, because Ave started touching himself, hand dropping to that hard on and stroking. Louis about choked to death and almost killed himself getting the rest off so he could get on the bed.

The blue fabric was as soft as it looked, making him hum at the feel of it rubbing his knees and Louis bent to cover Avery's body with his, kissing hard. Ave kissed right back, touching the nape of his neck, which sent electricity zinging through him, right to his cock. Louis reached right down between them and caught his cock and Ave's, bringing them together so they could slide and rock, the friction rolling up his spine and bursting in his head.

Ave's moan came deep and loud, almost shocking in its intensity, and they moved together like it was the first time; maybe it was. Maybe this was the first time for them in this new life they were creating together, so different from just throwing two people into the same house like they had before.

They rocked, Avery spreading beneath him, Louis pushing down between those long legs, panting. His sweat dropped on Avery's chest and his lips rained praise down on Avery's mouth. It was so good that he never wanted it to end, but too good to last much longer, and he opened his eyes to find Avery watching him, dazed, lips swollen and dark.

Avery's fingers twined into his messy curls and pulled him down, the kiss saying everything, I love you and I need you and thank God we're back together, and Louis knew because he felt the same damned way. He came hard, so hard, shooting wet and heat between them, crying out loud and happy. Ave followed close behind, gasping, hips pushing Louis up off the bed as he thrust into his orgasm, making them both groan with the strength of it.

They stayed like that for a long while, like both of them were afraid to speak and ruin the moment. Sooner or later, though, that kind of tension has to dissipate and Louis started laughing, making Avery whap him.

"What's so funny?"

"You think it will gross Justin right out if we tell him what a good job he did with the bed linens?"

Avery hooted. "Hell, yeah. I can't wait."

Neither could Louis.

Chapter Fourteen

The phone woke him at about eight on Sunday morning and Avery nudged Louis with his elbow, trying to get the big slug to answer the phone. He'd only been there a week, not hardly long enough for most anyone to be calling him, and if it was his mama or Justin they'd call his cell.

"Lou. Phone."

Louis just rolled away and snorted, his sleepy disgust evident, and Avery finally gave up and answered. "Louis' answering service."

"Oh. Hello?"

"Hello?" The voice sounded vaguely familiar and that he didn't place it right away was a sign of how sleepy Avery still was.

"Avery, honey? Is that you?"

Louis' mom. Goodness. "Yes ma'am. How are you?"

"I'm fine. Avery. I. Well, it's none of my business, but are you back for good?"

"Yes ma'am. I think I am."

"Oh, good. I'm so glad to hear it. Now could I speak to Louis, please."

"Sure. Hold on."

She'd never said so much as boo to him before, not really, and Avery couldn't help but feel good about the change as he whapped Louis with the phone to wake him up good and proper. Even Louis' mom approved. How could you beat that?

***

Louis answered the phone for what had to be the eight hundredth time that weekend and tried not to snarl. Between his mom and the folks who kept calling to find out if he and Avery were indeed back together he was getting downright anti-social.

"Hey, Lou. I heard."

Louis cut his friend Carl off at the pass. "Yeah. We are. We did. What?"

Carl chuckled. "Now don't snap at me, boy. I was just hoping it was true because Linda's been bitching we haven't had a decent game of pinochle since y'all broke up. When can you come over and play a bit?"

Something eased in his chest. Good old Carl, he never wanted to talk things out or gossip. He just wanted to be social. Louis had missed that. "When can Linda make some of those fine cheese sticks?"

"How about Sunday a week?"

That's the second best offer I've had in a long while, Carl. About three?"

"You bet. As long as you don't ever tell me what the first offer was."

"You got it."

***

The whole time they'd been apart Avery had dreamed of Louis' mouth. He'd dreamed about the way Louis kissed, the way he talked, and most importantly, how he sucked.

Louis was proving that all of that wistful longing hadn't made the memory better than the reality. Avery sat on the couch, legs spread wide as Louis licked and sucked and bobbed on his cock, his hands clenched in Louis' gorgeous, dark curls, looking down at that pink tongue as it swirled around the head of his prick.

"Lou."

"Mmm."

Yeah. Louis feasted on him, made sure he knew how much Louis liked his taste, his smell. There was never a doubt in his mind that Louis loved doing this for him, craved it as much as he did. And they could do it any time they wanted. Any old time.

Louis stroked Avery's balls, took Avery's cock deep, and as his back arched and his hips punched up with the force of his orgasm, Avery vowed never to take that for granted again. Ever.

***

They spent a lot of nights just snuggling on the couch, watching TV. Louis had always thought Avery was a champion snuggler, had always appreciated that about Ave, and tonight especially he was grateful for it. The last thing he wanted to do was chatter, or have to think hard enough to play board games.

Avery seemed drowsy and content, too, every so often making a comment about how hot the Indian guy was in Brotherhood of the Wolf, but otherwise letting him sip his beer and rest, which was just what he needed.

It was coming up on fall, which would be an off time for both him and Ave, at least until leaf raking season started, or maybe he should make that pine needle season around their neck of the woods, but still. Lou was working overtime, trying to get as much pay under his belt as he could, not just for the off season, but for the surprise he was trying to work up for Avery.

Trouble was it was making him grumpy as Hell and sore as a lion with a thorn in its paw, and man was he trying hard not to take it out on Avery, because yeah, last time that had worked so well, but sometimes it was nice to just have some peace and quiet.

Louis woke up about an hour later when Avery shook his shoulder and he blinked up into Ave's concerned gaze.

"You okay, Lou? You should get up and go to bed."

"Oh. Yeah, m'fine. Just a long day at work."

"Yeah. You looked so tired."

He knew Avery was fishing and knew he should probably just spill it, but he wanted so badly to keep the trip a secret, so he just rolled his shoulders and shook his head.

"I'll be fine, babe." He pecked a kiss on Ave's lips and headed for the bathroom. "Night."

"Night."

Louis could feel the weight of Avery's look all the way into the bedroom.

Could he help it if he wanted their first vacation together to be perfect?

***

Avery tripped over one of Louis' big shoes and swore, hopping around as his big toe throbbed. Fuck, that hurt.

For three weeks Louis had done really well, but it seemed like the more overtime Lou worked, the worse he got in the slob department. Avery swore up and down to himself that he wasn't going to confront Lou about it, because last time that had gotten him nothing but pain, but he couldn't deny the little feeling of panic that crept in on him.

Those bruised looking circles he dreaded had appeared under Louis' eyes again and the silences were getting longer and longer. Avery had tried to bring it up once and Louis had shrugged him off, and Avery wanted to scream, because they'd not even been living together a month or more and it was too soon for it to be going bad. Too, too soon.

So Avery packed that little kernel of fear back in the back of the closet with Louis' shoes and set to scrubbing the kitchen instead, and then maybe trimming back the roses now it was late summer and they had stopped blooming. If he worked hard enough he would forget it, at least for a while, and hopefully give Louis the space he needed. For whatever he needed it for.

***

"Goddamn it, Louis? Can't you pick up one fucking paper plate and put it in the trash? "

Louis looked up from his last piece of pizza and there was Avery, pissed as Hell and holding his plate and napkin, waving them about.

Fuck, he was tired.

"Sorry, Ave."

"Yeah. You always say that."

"Avery."

"Don't give me that long suffering shit."

"Fine." Louis got up, heading for the bedroom. "I'll take my long suffering ass to the shower. Don't worry, I'll make sure I don't leave a wet towel on your goddamn floor."

"Lou, please." Something about the tone of Avery's voice made him pause, back and shoulders tight, but willing to listen. "Please, I'm sorry. I just. I don't think I can do this again."

God. Lou closed his eyes before turning back to Avery and wading back into the fray. "Do what, Ave?"

"This thing. Where I watch you hurt and you don't talk to me and I'm afraid to ask and afraid not to."

"So it's all me."

"No!" And Avery didn't look mad, just scared. So scared and like he was gonna cry. "It's me, too. I don't know how to... I don't want to make you do anything you don't want to, Lou. But I thought. Well, I thought we were going to do better."

"We are. I'm just tired. I told you I'd tell you when I'm tired." Fuck, he didn't want to do this.

"I know. And I haven't pushed, have I?"

"No." To be fair, Ave hadn't, and this was the first time it had boiled over into other things. But when Louis thought about it, Avery had been slinking around the house, silent as a ghost instead, never bringing anything up and being way too content to just hold him while he slept. "I know you haven't."

"Then tell me what's going on. Please don't tell me it's none of my business."

"I need to sit."

"Okay."

He could tell Ave was trying not to hover and those hands were just twisting that paper plate in front of Avery's belly, showing off the case of nerves Ave had. Louis sighed.

"Would you come here and sit?"

Avery sat, relief flashing in his eyes, hand coming out to rest on Louis' leg, fingers petting lightly. Louis let the touch soothe him; let it calm him. Keeping the trip a secret from Avery was backfiring on him, because Ave could tell he wasn't talking, but not why. The way he was perched on the sofa spoke of nothing more than dread.

"I'm sore. I've been working too much. But it's not to get away from you or because I'm going to have to switch jobs again or anything."

"So why?'

"Babe..." Louis sucked it up and just fucking told Ave. Fuck it if it spoiled it. "I've been saving up. I, um. I bought us tickets to Florida in September. So we could have that vacation we wanted."

"You. You did this so we could have a vacation."

Oh, shit. That was a scowl, not a smile. Ave looked *pissed*. Well. That would teach him to do something like that ever again.

"I just wanted to do something nice."

"Oh, babe. Didn't you think it might be too early in this whole living together thing to go all silent on me again? Jesus, I was scared you'd decided you'd made a mistake and you were working overtime and going to bed early at night to avoid me. I was wracking my brain trying to think what I had done to make you so angry, and so damned tired. Louis, this is what happened the first time. You have to talk to me."

"And you have to learn to ask."

Okay, maybe that was petty, but it was true. Louis couldn't handle the whole Christian martyr thing again.

"The last time I asked you told me it was none of my business and to get out."

"Yeah, well it was the way you asked."

Exhausted, Louis leaned back against the soft couch cushion and closed his eyes. He was so fucking tired and he knew he had screwed up. He always did, because he always just thought he could shoulder everything alone, pull up his socks and just do it. Avery deserved better than that, though. He deserved to be in on everything.

"I'm sorry, babe."

"Me, too, Louis. Just, please, promise you'll try. And I will, too, I swear. I was just so scared."

Avery pressed up against him, warm and good, and Louis relaxed, breath leaving him in a rush. He hadn't fucked up as bad as all that if Avery wanted to snuggle. Unless it was more of the I don't know how to ask petting.

"I will. You don't have to hold me if you're mad."

"I'm not. Look at me."

He opened his eyes, seeing nothing but sweet relief and a healthy dose of loving. Louis smiled, sliding his arms around Avery's waist. "You're not gonna run away?"

"No. You won't kick me out?"

"Hell, no."

"Good. The rest we can talk about later. Let's get you to bed."

"I don't have to…"

Avery moved, pulled him up off the couch and herded him. "Yeah, you do. And if you want you could tell your boss no more overtime."

"I could do that." He could. He'd rather make things right with Avery than go to Florida, come to that.

"Good. We can talk vacation plans this weekend."

"We can."

Maybe that was something to look forward to. Maybe that would be even better than a nice surprise. Doing it together.

***

Avery watched Louis sleep, brushing his fingers across the dark circles under Louis' eyes, torn between beating him to death and kissing him until he woke up and did the nasty with him.

He settled for petting and trying to let go of the tension that made his shoulders tight and his head hurt. Damn it, he should be able to; they'd talked it out. He just couldn't. There was some hard thinking to do, because Avery wasn't sure he could do this kind of up and down for the rest of his life.

Did he want the rest of his life with Louis? Hell yes, he did. He loved Louis like no one else and hard as the man was to live with, Avery knew there was no one else for him. But could he handle the pins and needles and tiptoeing over eggshells?

Of course, Louis could be right. It could be the way he asked, waiting until something else made it explode and snapping Lou's head off. That was at least as passive aggressive as Lou holding it all inside and not letting him help, wasn't it? God, it was depressing to think they had come so far and then see that they still had the same shit to work out.

Maybe they were working on it, though. Hadn't they finally sat down and talked, with Lou telling him what was going on? That had to be a first. And...

"I hope that's a gray hair you're trying to pull out because otherwise I like my follicles unmolested."

Surprised, Avery tugged on Louis' hair even harder when he jumped, making Lou yelp. "Shit! Sorry, babe."

"S'okay. I can tell when I'm being punished."

For that he whapped Louis on the head, meaning to sting this time. "I was just petting."

"You weren't sleeping."

"No. I couldn't."

Rolling up, Louis propped on his elbows and looked at Ave, hair standing out everywhichways. "I'm sorry."

"It's okay, Lou. We're getting there."

They were. He knew they were. Lou didn't say anything else, Lou never did if the man could help it, just leaned up and kissed him, gentle and sweet and apologetic. Avery kissed him back gratefully, tongue pushing into Louis' mouth, tasting, loving. Telling Lou it was all right.

They loved slow, easy, touches light enough to tease, murmuring to each other, silly love words. It was so not like them and Avery wasn't sure what to make of it, but it felt so damned good that he finally gave up trying to figure it out.

He'd figure it all out in the morning.

***

Louis came home early the next day, having told the boss he was through doing overtime and getting a curt, "About time," barked at him.

Sometimes he wondered if he really was that much of an asshole when he was tired and grumpy. Yeah, okay, he'd bet he was.

Stopping on his way home, Louis picked up a London broil to cook for dinner, along with squash casserole and fresh corn. He got everything cooking in the oven, turned up the a/c to account for it, then went and got all of his brochures and tickets and shit for Florida.

He and Avery could sit and plan their vacation out together. Like they should have in the first place.

Sometimes you could teach old dogs new tricks after all.

Avery got home just in time to save the meat from overcooking and to give him the kiss he so desperately needed, hands holding his hips and pulling him close.

"You? Look a hundred percent better, Lou."

"I had a nap. My boss told me I was being an asshole."

Avery laughed, leaning against him and holding him tight. "You were. So was I."

"It's not like it will never happen again."

He wanted to make sure that was clear to both of them. Life was never going to be all smooth sailing, or whatever. They were just too different for it to always be easy.

"Yeah, but if last night is any indication? We're finally learning to deal with it."

That was true enough. Louis thought it was a damned good start, which sounded silly with all of their history, but nobody was perfect, right?

"Come on and help me plan our vacation."

Epilogue

Florida was… well, wet. The day they'd showed up it had started raining and it hadn't stopped the whole first two days. Avery had cheerfully ignored it, buying them both ugly, fish printed umbrellas and trekking from tourist trap to tourist trap, happy as a clam in mud. It was as endearing as it was annoying.

On the third morning Louis got up and looked out at the cloudy sky, sighed, and decided to order room service and stay in bed no matter what Avery wanted to do. If it didn't stop by the end of the week? He was gonna be pissed.

"Hey."

Louis looked over at Avery, who was climbing out of bed, naked mind you, and coming over to press right up against him, all sleep warm and blinky.

"Hey. It's still raining. I ordered room service."

"Oh, cool! I've never had room service."

Damn. Avery was so happy that Louis hated to be so grumpy. He just couldn't help it. Fucking rain.

"Well, now you will."

"Come back to bed with me until it shows."

Julia Talbot

Ave tugged on his hand and he went, but reluctantly. He wasn't sure he wanted to snuggle. He might infect Avery with the doldrums. They sat down together and Ave pushed at him until he toppled over and Avery could straddle his thighs and grin down at him.

"All right, sourpuss. What's got you so pissy?"

"The fucking rain. It's ruining our vacation."

"Is it? I thought we were doing really well. I'm having fun."

He knew pouting was probably damned unattractive, but he was doing it anyway. "Good."

"Look. The hotel is gorgeous, right?"

It was. Their room had an old world ambiance, with antique-y looking furniture and pretty striped wallpaper, and their bathroom had a whirlpool big enough for two.

"Yeah. It is."

"And the meals have been exquisite."

"Sure." They'd splurged on surf and turf one night and on fancy Italian food the other. Hell, even breakfast and lunch had been good.

"And with a lot of the stuff we've done we'd just get wet anyway."

A smile pulled at his lips, even though Louis tried to stifle it. Avery was making it impossible to stay upset. "Yeah, yeah, okay. It's been good. I just. Well, I wanted it to be perfect for us."

Those whiskey eyes he loved stared right down into his, Avery going serious in a heartbeat. Avery touched his cheek, leaned down to kiss his mouth, slow and deep and sizzling.

"If there's one thing I've learned in the last year, babe? It's that love doesn't have to be perfect. It just has to be us."

Oh. Louis pulled Avery back down, pouring all of his love and wonder into their next kiss. That? He could live with. For the rest of his life.

End

LaVergne, TN USA
13 November 2009
164055LV00001B/38/A